Golden Mile

Gem Burman

For my hometown: Great Yarmouth.

My story began there, and this one does too.

"Sometimes in the waves of change,
we find our true direction."
UNKNOWN

Contents

Batten Down the Hatches

Prologue

June 2021

'Afternoon madam, we're looking for Mr. Blewitt,' came an authoritative gruff voice from out of nowhere.

The petite, bemused-looking brunette's head shot up from behind the lounge bar. Nobody usually asked for Mr. Blewitt … and if they did, they'd have difficulty keeping a straight face. People mostly asked to check in in sunny voices. If they were checking out, it'd be a bit more on the pissed-off side but generally, formal, scary voices weren't the norm around here.

She did a double take at the two policemen standing before her and gulped hard. The Old Bill asking after you is never good – well, not unless it's a strip show. But these two didn't look like they were about to whip out their love truncheons at any moment, which, given that they were both beastly-looking behemoths, was a blessing. Their body language suggested they hadn't come to warn that there had been a spate of burglaries in the area, either. No, this was personal. She froze, mind whirling like the Pleasure Beach carousel.

'Um, I'm Mrs. Blewitt … Sharon Blewitt,' she answered, inwardly cringing. God, that bloody surname! Even though she'd acquired it two decades ago, hearing it spoken out loud was just as toe-curling as it had always been.

She felt her pulse kick as the beeps and distorted unintelligible ramblings from their police radios took her back to the early nineties when Becky 'Bex' Armstrong nicked a bottle of Charlie Red from Superdrug and tried to pin it all on her. Still, she'd heard about Becky's lifetime ban from Poundland recently, which brought her some comfort.

In all her forty-one years, *Charliegate* had been Sharon Blewitt's one and only brush with the law – if you could call it that – and even then, she was bloody innocent.

A highly intuitive inkling told her that Pat the Donut Lady was watching with saucer eyes, and, sure enough, upon craning her neck toward the front bay window which looked out onto the bustling seafront, there was Pat, crammed inside her little pink hut with her annoying, large head looking straight toward the B&B. Her eyes would've been out on stalks the second the police car drew up.

Pat was reputed the town over for her donuts

which were hot, fresh and had that perfect *crisp* to the batter every time … but she was also known for her big gob; a gob that jangled more than her tawdry jewellery collection which she tended to wear all at once. A gob that twittered louder than the brassy bird's nest she favoured for a hairdo. The woman had more scoop than the Eastern Daily Press and what Pat knew, everyone got to find out. Even with a mile-long queue, she was always on the qui vive, fishing for gossip with one beady eye on the donut machine and the other on the comings and goings outside. Guaranteed, she'd be messing herself in excitement over this!

Both officers' gazes flipped conjointly toward the doorway as her husband, Gary, emerged whistling "I Do Like to Be Beside the Seaside." He trailed off and went all stiff and serious as though he'd tried for a silent fart and followed through.

A fraught silence ensued, and Sharon watched a look of guilt etch its way across the face she'd known since her teens. It was the same look he'd have when a *right sort* walked past in town, or when she opened the Quality Street tin at Christmas and lost her shit because all the green triangles had gone already. Except that this was far more unnerving. This was serious. She sort of guessed that from the way the colour seemed to drain from his face all at once. He looked like he'd seen a bloody ghost!

'Mr. Blewitt? Gary Blewitt?'

'Don't tell me, Ma's gone and snuffed it!' He

3

laughed, nervously.

Chance would be a fine thing, Sharon thought.

Both officers remained straight-faced. 'I'm going to need you to accompany us to the station for questioning, sir,' said one of them.

Gary's mouth went into an unattractive spasm which didn't do much for his sex appeal. If he was going to be arrested in public, he could've at least tried to look a bit sexy; like Tom Cruise in "Mission Impossible 3." Tom had it bang-on with the sexy furrowed brow and slight look of confusion intermingled with an overall self-assured masculinity and good hair. He lost it a little at the point he got tasered and started twitching on the ground, but he still looked hot, Sharon thought – unlike Gary who stood frozen in terror like a crap Paul Hollywood waxwork forged by the old Louis Tussauds House of Wax.

'W-why? What for?' He stammered.

The police officer peered toward the outside foyer, observing the small group of perplexed holidaymakers that had just arrived, their eyes darting speculatively from the policemen, to Gary, to Sharon, and back.

'It's probably going to be best if we explain everything out in the car, sir.'

Gary nodded, defeatedly. 'Back soon, baby,' he mumbled ashen faced.

A pang of anxiety coursed through Sharon's stomach as she caught the knowing look exchanged between the two policemen which seemed to suggest otherwise. What in the hell was going on? Whatever it was, it was serious. Of that, she was certain.

The other policeman turned his attention to her. 'Is there anyone who can look after things here? We'll need you to come down to the station to answer some questions yourself.'

'Are we under arrest?' She gasped with a nervous laugh.

He hesitated a little too long for her liking. 'For now, we're asking you to come to the station voluntarily to help us with our enquiries, madam. But it does need to be today,' he added, sternly.

She nodded. 'I'll sort some cover and pop down as soon as possible.' *Pop down?* Jeez! You could tell how often she had dealings with the police!

She watched as Gary sloped off, turning, and giving her a woeful last glance as though he were being led to the gallows. *I'll kill him! I'll bloody kill him! What's he gone and done?!*

Shaking her head in disbelief, she gripped the edge of the bar for support, half-expecting to wake from a really shit dream. This sort of thing didn't happen to the Blewitts. Gary didn't have run-ins with the police, he was far too boring! They were just a cosy seaside B&B along Great Yarmouth's seafront rated five on Tripadvisor. And this was the Norfolk coast, not The Bronx. It was madness. Utter madness!

Quite how she went on to check in the waiting guests without incident, she didn't know. Whilst she had been careful to retain her dynamic-local-businesswoman voice, on the inside she was, to be frank, absolutely crapping her pants.

The Blewitts had come so far in recent times. They'd been treading water most of their married lives until, eventually, with a little help from Lady Luck, they caught the wave that is life. Admittedly, it'd all felt too good to be true for Sharon as they rode the surf like pros, such that a small part of her was always bracing herself for the wipe-out. Was this it? Had Lady Luck decided to give them the middle finger?

Sharon didn't have a clue as to why the police would turn up unannounced to summon them to the station for questioning, but she couldn't shake the feeling that Gary did.

Down in the Doldrums

Chapter 1

Summer 2019

'Who was that Apple founder, again?' Sharon asked her husband as they lay in bed together one muggy Sunday night.

Gary turned his head toward her in slack-jawed confusion. 'Granny Smith?'

'Don't be daft! I mean, Him! The techie bloke. The Apple dude.' They'd been married twenty years, surely, he should be able to read her thoughts by now.

'Oh, you mean Steve Jobs?' Hallelujah! There was hope for them yet.

'That's the one. What was it he said, again?'

'How the chuff am I supposed to know?! Could be bloody anything!'

With a sigh, Sharon swiped her phone from atop the bedside chest of drawers and consulted the one candidate she could be sure would know what she was looking for: Google. 'Steve Jobs quotes,' she muttered out loud. 'That's it! *If today were the last day of my life, would I want to do what I am about to do today? Whenever the answer is no for too many days in a row, I know I need to change something.*' This was her hint that she wanted to live and not just exist. For too long, it'd felt like everyone else was having a ball and the Blewitts were NFI'd (not fucking invited); their noses pressed against the glass as the world partied on. For a long time, she'd ignored it. Just got on with it. But now, her acute awareness of the clock ticking and the sands of time draining away was keeping her up at night. The treadmill of life was moving but she was going nowhere, while somehow at the same time, careering toward the Big Four-0. And with the average life expectancy in the United Kingdom 81.2 years, this suggested that half her life was up already without her noticing. It was as though she'd been stood on the promenade with a full bag of chips, turned her head for a moment and some big, bastard seagull had come along and snatched half in one fell swoop. Now all she had left was a handful of decent ones among the shrivelled dredges and crispy bits. *What if I were to die tomorrow? What would my legacy be?* She asked herself continually: a filthy oven, a full laundry basket and a five grand funeral bill at this rate!

A chink of streetlight seeped through the gap in the curtains enough for her to observe Gary's vacant expression.

Glumly, she rolled over to face him. 'Do you ever

feel like you've come to a crossroads in life, Gaz?'

He stared at her, nonplussed. *Obviously not!*

'You know, When I was a kid, people always used to ask me what I wanted to be when I grew up. I didn't really know. All I knew was that I was going to be somebody. I'd be my own boss, live in a big house by the sea and be able to buy whatever I wanted. I was so sure of it back then. It was as though it were written in stone.'

He gave a loud snort. 'Well, I'll say one thing for you Shaz, you're no Nostradamus.'

She followed his gaze up toward the gaping hole in the corner of the ceiling that had been there for months. 'Well, we do live in a seaside town.'

'Yeah, in a two-bed terrace that's falling to bits,' he reminded her. 'Anyway, I've gotta be up for six, I'll be buggered if I'm wasting valuable sleeping time talking about things we can't change. Night, baby.' With that, he rolled over and, within the space of a few minutes, was snoring like a Great Dane with a chronic lung condition.

It wasn't often that Sharon attempted heart-to-hearts with her husband, but when she did, she got more conversation out of the wall. It irked her that their problems felt as though they were all hers; that Gary slept like a log while she lay wide awake until the small hours doing his share of the worrying for him:

How are we going to make six quid last till payday? Will the electric company hold out for another

9

week?
What kind of day will I have at work tomorrow?
I'm going grey!
The best years of my life are over already!
Gaz and I haven't 'done it' in weeks!

Only a true insomniac can appreciate how desperately lonely it is in the middle of the night when all but your thoughts has come to a standstill. The mind becomes a relentless conveyor belt of worries amplified tenfold by the silent still of the early hours.

It hadn't always been like this. In the beginning, they'd gone together like *rama-lama-lama-ka-dinga-da-dinga-dong.* They wanted the same things. The trouble was – as Sharon was later to find out – Gary wanted it all on a plate. Like anyone, he would quite happily have filled his boots with all the world had to offer, provided it would be delivered to his door in an Amazon van. The nearest he had to 'get-up-and-go' these days was when he'd get up and go to the pub. He seemed quite happy to bob along in life in the same job he'd had ever since he'd left school.

'But don't you want to be more than just a forklift driver, though?' Sharon asked him, time and time again, to which he'd shrug and reply *with power comes great responsibility.* Gary Blewitt was a man who liked to keep things simple; the simpler the better. But this only seemed to apply to things like work, DIY, bedroom athletics and pretty much anything that required him to move his arse. The same certainly didn't apply at tea times when the Blewitts sat down to another banquet of whatever was left in the freezer. *Thank you, lord, for this wonderful food we're about to eat; fucking fish fingers again*, he'd complain. It never occurred to him that he had the power to change it. He seemed to just accept that this was it for them. But Sharon's hunger went far beyond the dinner table. She craved success, free-living and financial freedom; lost herself in daydreams of holidays abroad, romantic weekends away and fun-filled family days out. She could only cling like a limpet to the hope that, even with the Gary-shaped anchor holding it back and a bloody great hole in the hull, their ship would one day come in.

'YEOUCH! GET OFF, MUM!' Izzy yelled, making Sharon jump as she styled her hair for school the next morning.

'Sorry, did I comb your face again?' The question was answered with a snake-like hiss and a look of contempt.

Although she knew the fishtail braid she was cleverly constructing while staring into space would be long gone come home time, and in its place, a bedraggled mop à la Stig of The Dump, Sharon still strived to send their daughter to school just as well turned out as everyone else. The Blewitts were just as good as any other family – though it didn't feel that way when they were forced to utilise The Advertiser as bog roll, cut open the tube to get to the last of the toothpaste and pray to God that Izzy didn't lose any more teeth because the tooth fairy was still in debt to her for the last lot!

Money was tighter than Madonna's forehead, and while it's certainly true that it doesn't bring you happiness, neither does being skint. Sharon had often heard it said that there are positives to be found in every situation. The only one she could draw from being permanently brassic was the unrivalled protection from bank fraud it offered: nobody can nick what isn't there.

'DAH! YOU GOT IT IN MY EYES!' Izzy roared as Sharon finished up the braid with a liberal spritz of hairspray in bold hopes that the fifty-nine pence investment would make for a day-long, neat child.

'But I covered them with my hands?'

'You covered everything except my eyes!'

'Oh. Sorry.'

This was what she'd been reduced to these days: a permanently zoned out, starey prisoner of her own mind. She had the dreamer's disease. Her head was always somewhere else: sometimes in the past, mostly in the future, but rarely in the present.

'What about *Number Day*?' Izzy suddenly piped up halfway to school.

'Sorry, sweetie?'

'Today is *Come To School Dressed as a Number Day*,' she repeated, wearily.

Sharon froze in horror, stomach dropping the way it always did when she'd forgotten about *World Book Day*, *Easter Bonnet Day*, *Odd Socks Day* and every other bloody day the South Shore Primary PTA dreamed up to task embattled parents with.

Oh my God! I'm the worst mum in the world, second to Kate McCallister in "Home Alone"!

Not even her distinction in fishtail braids could save her now. She'd ballsed up ... again.

'Why didn't you tell me this before we left?! You should've told me before we left!' She wailed, pulling her hands through her sun-kissed brown ponytail.

'I ain't a reminder service!' Izzy cheeked.

'Well ... why don't you just say you've come as yourself because you're *number one*?'

Izzy scowled back at her mother, unimpressed. 'Because that would be number twos!'

Arriving out of breath at the clothing section in Sainsburys, Sharon grabbed a salmon-pink hoodie emblazoned with a random US state and the number eighty-five and raced to the checkout. It was a sickening waste of money, and the cashier did well to disguise her WTF-face as they entered a strange tug of war over the £20 note Sharon couldn't bear to give up from her grasp. With a strangled whimper, she eventually let go. At least Izzy wouldn't be the only one still in uniform this time: problem solved. Except, it wasn't, really. Fourteen quid down the Swanee and now running late, Sharon had two new problems. Ah, well. They'd just have to juggle things. Sharon was an ace juggler from years of penny-pinching, but she was only ever a few quid off dropping the balls.

The pavements in proximity of the school were crammed with the same SUVs and people carriers that would arrive super-early to ensure their space – all of them strangely grey as though this was their equivalent to the Pink Ladies jacket for *The Godmothers* – the name by which Sharon secretly referred to the cartel of cliquey mums that ruled the playground at South Shore Primary. Most of their husbands worked on the rigs so they lived for the school runs which had become a social event to get up and pour themselves into yoga pants for – gym wear was another symbol of membership, the brighter the better – and although they were giving off the impression that they were fitness freaks, none of them had arses to vouch for it. The only thing you could be sure got a bloody good workout was their gobs as they stood blocking the school gates every morning and afternoon, stopping everyone else from getting their kids in and out while they stood wildly gesticulating with their arms and gassing for Britain. Sharon would never get so much as a vague look in her direction. As far as The Godmothers were concerned, anyone with a household income of less than fifty grand per annum wasn't worth a highly pitched, fake-ass *Hiiiiiiyaaaaaa!*

With number eighty-five dispatched off to school later than planned, Sharon could now afford to run all the way to work Captain-Jack-Sparrow-style. All she could hear was The Boomtown Rats' "I don't like Mondays," as she ran like hell in the shabby loafers she'd coloured-in with permanent marker to disguise the scuffs. She couldn't do anything about the unevenly-worn-down heels, though, which is why she was running like a tit.

The muddled smell of cheap home fragrance, plastics and new rugs told her she'd arrived in the discount homewares store that she seemed to spend her life in.

She'd barely made it more than a metre inside before Dawn – supervisor and power-hungry jobsworth extraordinaire – sprang out from behind a giant gold ornamental buddha head. 'You're late!'

Yep, it was just another day in paradise!

Sharon frowned down at her watch. 'But it's only 8.57?'

Dawn folded her arms behind her back the way she always did when she was trying to be authoritative. 'And that would make you seven minutes late, Sharon. As you know, we like staff to arrive at least ten minutes before the start of every shift. A little courtesy's all we ask. It's not hard.'

Question: What do you get if you combine every cinema wrapper rustler on the planet, every wet mouth sound you ever heard, every driver who drove so far up your arse that they might as well be your passenger, every snotty GP surgery receptionist you've ever dealt with and the worst case of vaginal thrush ever?
Answer: The smallest idea of how annoying Dawn Turner is!

If being a pain in the arse were an Olympic sport, Dawn would take gold, there's no doubt about it. Sharon considered herself an easy-going person with near- endless calm and patience, but Dawn had a unique way of making her want to rip her eyeballs out of her skull within seconds of speaking to her. Was it the way she seemed to glide instead of walk? Her daft glasses that looked like they came from the joke shop down Regent Road … the ones which make your eyes look massive? The way she talked through her nose? The way she slurped her tea from the ridiculous Wallace and Gromit mug she drank out of in the staff room believing it was cool? It was everything about the bloody woman. Sharon would be dead before she could list her annoying traits in their entirety. Still, there was no point explaining she'd had a mad morning because the Fifty-something-year-old Wallace and Gromit fan had never been married and didn't have kids. She wasn't going to appreciate the ball-ache of *Come to School Dressed as a Number Day*. Accordingly, Sharon neglected to mention it.

'It won't happen again,' she muttered, indignantly.

'You betcha, it won't!' Dawn sneered after her as she raced up the escalator to the staff room to put her bag away. Along the way, Sharon made a mental note to get the hell on Indeed when she got home to find survivable alternative employment, recalled that her last search at 3am that morning produced nothing new except a vacancy for a dog walker, then paused in actual consideration of it...

Pros:

Dogs don't micromanage

Dogs don't talk through their noses

Dogs don't make you spend the whole day fantasising about beating them with an entire range of non-stick frying pans.

Cons:

Dogs tend to shit. *Gag!*

'Ah, Sharon! Glad I bumped into you ... *literally*,' her colleague, Penny, chortled as she ploughed straight into her on her way out of the staff room.

Sharon felt a gloomy sense of Déjà vu wash over her, the kind you get when you know you're about to be left worse off in some way – like when you answer your phone to an unknown caller, and they start the conversation with *how are you today?*

'I'm doing a collection for Anne's leaving present. We're getting her some vouchers for her favourite garden centre. Fiver each. Will you be putting in?'

Chuff, me! Sharon thought. Another collection? *I only just put in a fiver for Natalie-from-the-cash-office-who-I-don't-even-know's baby shower gift! And Anne? Anne? Who the hell's Anne?! Sod off with your collections! I'm skint! I need you to all do a collection for me just to get by!* She summoned her sweetest voice. 'Yeah, sure. When do you need the money by?'

'Today would be perfect if that's okay?'

It was bloody far from okay, but, once again, Sharon found herself rooting through her purse with a smile that was already making her face ache, counting out a fiver from the change from the hoodie, and handing it over as though she wouldn't miss it. *Go on, have it! Have it! It's only my last fiver, but hey, Anne's garden comes first.*

'Great, I'll mark you off the list,' Penny chirped.

It was around twenty minutes later that Sharon realised the precedent had been set for the day from hell when an old dear brought fifty individual pieces of cutlery to her till, handing each item over to be scanned slower than a snail on tranquilisers as, ironically, Louis Armstrong's "We Have All the Time in the World" played away quietly in the background on the store radio.

Sharon could see Dawn out of the corner of her eye, flouncing up and down, talking frantically into her headset as the queue lengthened. *Jesus H. Christ! A queue! There's only a bloody quuuuuuuueue! In a shop, of all places.*

Moments later, the cavalry arrived, and Dawn directed them to the tills as though they were all blind. Of course, she could've just hopped on a till herself to help, but that would've meant passing up the opportunity to use that poncy headset of hers – not just a headset, but also a symbol of her authority and superiority. Sharon doubted she was talking to anyone half the time she used it.

An eternity later, the last item of cutlery was scanned. 'That'll be seventy-four pounds fifty please,' Sharon announced, almost nodding off as the old dear fished her debit card out of her purse, battled to get it into the slot in the card machine, and then stood there for an age trying to remember her pin. She gave it a few tries and stood scratching her head as it rejected each time. 'Ooh, er ... err. Now, then. What could it be?'

Don't look at me, love. I have a job remembering my own!

Eventually, she must've had a memory flash because the transaction went through and the till drawer flew open, hitting Sharon in the noonie. 'There y'are, that's you all done.' She winced, nudging the carrier bag of cutlery toward her.

The old dear didn't move, just stood there with her glasses perched on the end of her nose staring hard at her receipt.

'Er … is there a problem?'

'Should they be that expensive, dear? I calculated it to come to seventy-two pounds-fifty.'

Sharon glanced at the till screen. 'Er, no. They're one pound forty-nine each and you've got fifty pieces there. That's seventy-four-pounds and fifty pence.'

'Oh. Oh. Well then, I don't want them, dear. Could I have a refund?'

Seriously? For two scabby quid? It was all Sharon could do not to lean across the counter, grab her in a chokehold, and throttle her Homer-Simpson-style!

No sooner had the flurry of customers been served, than Dawn was already gliding toward Sharon's till in her own unique way, addressing her as though she were a five-year-old. 'Could we perhaps make ourselves useful and go and re-stock the shelves? Time is money, darling!'

Sharon glanced at the giant wooden storage trunk to her side, longing to push her in and close the lid. 'No problem, Dawn. There won't be anyone on the tills though.'

'You'll be called if you're needed on the tills,' Dawn muttered, icily, before, less than two minutes later, calling Sharon straight back to the tills … then dismissing her to stack shelves … then calling her back to the tills. God forbid that she might stand still for a few seconds because then the business wouldn't be getting maximum productivity out of their staff in return for their meagre minimum wage investment. It was like *from you, we expect the world, from us you can expect the minimum we can get away with paying you.*

There was a dossier of things Sharon hated about her job, but the way Dawn announced *you're free to go* at the end of each shift in her Zippy-from-Rainbow voice trounced the lot. She would keep everybody waiting like school kids while she fannied about doing nothing much, just to remind them all that she was in charge and that their leaving to go home to their families depended on her say so. If she caught the slightest tut or eye roll, she'd take even longer.

As Sharon recalled, nowhere in her childhood daydreams did she foresee thirty-nine-year-old her, standing around with bated breath waiting for some Anne Robinson lookalike of unsound mind to grant her permission to breathe. She had to get out of there! To find a way to change her life beyond buying the odd lottery ticket and fully expecting to win.

The Wicked Witch of the West's theme tune immediately sprung to mind as Sharon turned the corner into Beaconsfield Road to find the mother-in-law's car parked outside her house: a Fiat 500 in what she liked to call *contemporary nude* but what was better described as hearing aid beige.

Great. From one giant pain in the arse to another! Sharon thought, mentally debating who was worse. *Stella or Dawn? Dawn or Stella?* Well, that was as good a comparison as Chlamydia and Gonorrhoea!

To describe someone like Stella Payne would take all day, so imagining a sulky blobfish with smoker's lines and one of those supposed-to-make-you-look-trendy-but-adds-years-to-you dyed grey bobs would be a good place to start. You could go further by imagining its reflection in the back of a spoon. And further still by imagining the put-on limp invented to get a disabled parking badge – which had been known to disappear like magic on occasions such as the Next sale.

There was only two rules Stella lived her life by:

Rule 1: It's all about Stella.
Rule 2: In the rare event that it is not all about Stella, refer to rule 1.

Sharon could be talking about her feet hurting from work and before she'd get to finish her sentence, they'd suddenly be talking about Stella's Arthritis. She habitually monopolised every conversation, so it was easier all round just to switch off and let her rock-on, running her mouth and dramatically bursting into tears for attention.

You knew it was coming when her abrasive, whiny voice would suddenly dip to a whisper and she'd bring a quivering hand up to her face, dramatically clasping her mouth as though she'd just been given weeks to live. Every visit was like sitting through a crap pantomime.

Though she'd never met him, Sharon could quite understand why Gary's dad buggered off thirty-odd years ago and Stella had been single ever since. But with no significant other in her life and time on her hands, this gave her all the time in the world to smother the Blewitts with impromptu visits, crack-of-dawn phone calls, self-invites and pity plays – though it was only Gary she wanted; not out of healthy, motherly love, but her desperate need to keep him close. Sharon felt sure that Stella would have loved nothing more than for her and Izzy to be out of the picture so that mother and son could live alone together as if there was no one else in the world, like Norma and Norman Bates in *Psycho*.

Fittingly, Stella's maiden name which she'd reverted to after the divorce was *Payne*, which Sharon's folks found amusing. *She's lucky this ain't Australia*, her dad, Jim, would say, *'cos when folk say her name it'd sound like still a pain.* And so, her secret nickname was born and, as her Eeyorish mithering resonated from behind the sitting room door, Sharon was reminded of just how fitting it was. 'Well, he's put me on these blood pressure pills and they're making me feel ever so weak and dizzy,' she complained, pausing part-way to cough for effect.

Then why don't you sod off home?! Sharon thought.

''Ello, baby,' Gary muttered, not looking up from the sofa as she wafted into the front room.

Izzy remained glued to her iPad.

Stella, who sat looking pissed-off in polka dots in the chair by the window, fell silent and stared through Sharon as though she'd ceased to exist, then picked up where she'd left off. 'Yes, well I've been advised to take it easy, start looking after myself.' Given that this was all the old boot had ever done, the statement was somewhat of a joke.

Sharon usually asked people how they were when she first saw them, but she never bothered with Stella because she was permanently 'in the wars' so there was no point. She plonked herself on the sofa arm beside Gary. 'Hey, I was thinking since I finish off at four this Saturday, why don't you and Izzy meet me in town? We don't have to spend any money. We could just go for a beach walk, grab an icecr—'

'Can't, baby. I'm in Sheffield for me pool tournament,' he cut-in, crisply.

Sharon emitted an exasperated sigh. 'Not another one!'

Stella's head turned sharply toward her. 'Leave him alone! Let the poor man enjoy himself.'

Sharon stared back at her in disbelief. 'Oh, believe me, I do, Stella. He was away the week before last and the week before that!'

Stella raised a sparse brow which had been shakily overdrawn in some weird shade of pink-brown pencil. It left Sharon wondering whether her mother-in-law knew the difference between her brows and her lips.

'Good golly, you're not sewn at the hip. Let him breathe, woman!' Stella hissed.

It was hard to keep a lid on the pent-up, expletive-ridden, casserole of home truths threatening to spill out of Sharon's mouth. She and Gary had often had many a blazing row over the pool tournaments he played in up and down the country, and Stella just loved to fan the flames. She was the devil on his shoulder, encouraging his little adventures away from home and slipping him the cash to pay for it, because unless Gary had been allowed to pay for everything with Monopoly money, he wasn't paying himself.

'It's me passion, innit?' He excused with a nonchalant shrug.

Ah, yes: *passions.* Sharon had those, too, languishing somewhere at the back of a long queue of priorities. She threw him a look that told him they'd pick up with this over turkey dinosaurs once the she-devil had buggered off home, which, given the awkward silence, Sharon hoped would be any second now. She held her breath in hope as Stella moved to speak.

'I think Izzy has allergies.' *Ba-dum tish!*

Sharon looked at her, gone out. 'Pardon?'

'Her eyes look red.'

'That's probably because she's never off that thing,' she reasoned, motioning toward the tablet Izzy was sprawled on the carpet tapping away frantically upon.

'I really don't think so,' Stella persisted. 'I have allergies myself, so I know what hay fever looks like.'

Sharon glanced at Gary who was engrossed in his phone. 'What do you think, Gaz?'

'Hmmmmmm?'

'Do you think Izzy has hay fever?'

'Yeah, great, baby.'

With her husband about as much help as a dissolving condom, Sharon sought to quickly shut this down. 'I'll get her an appointment at the surgery. See what the doctor thinks.'

'Don't be silly, you'll not get an appointment for weeks! Don't have the poor girl suffer, get her sorted now. Get down to the walk-in centre.'

Sharon glanced downward in dismay at Izzy who was fully engrossed in her game and grinning her head off. It was after six on a school night. The last thing she needed was to rush down to the walk-in centre to sit staring at the same flu jab poster for a few hours for no good reason beyond having a hypochondriac in the family who, not satisfied enough with inventing her own illnesses, liked to invent them for everyone else, too.

Stella stared back at her, expectantly; her sullen trout-face twitching in eager anticipation of another medical dilemma.

'There's really no need,' Sharon mumbled, fully confident that Izzy was no more a sufferer of hay fever than Stella was of ninety-nine per cent of the illnesses she'd had over the past year. *She* knew her daughter best.

With an expression akin to having trodden barefoot on a jellyfish, a scornful sneer escaped Stella's thin, pursed lips. 'Well, there's no helping those who won't help themselves.'

Rather than smothering her mother-in-law with the sausage dog neck support pillow she took with her wherever she went, Sharon bit her lip and flounced off toward the kitchen when, still within earshot, Stella muttered 'she's never been mother material.'

Seething, Sharon yanked open the fridge door as though it were Stella's head, wondering – in terms of both the lone bulb of garlic inside and life in general – *is this it?* They say that happiness is a state of mind, but that couldn't be right. How could she be happy with this? No. Happiness was a destination. Some parallel universe out there waiting for her behind a hidden door. A place where problems didn't exist, all was well, and life was carefree. What would it look like behind this hidden door? How would she find it? She didn't know, but all she had to do was make it there and everything would come good. Life would be perfect.

But for now, there was only two things to do:

1. Get the turkey dinosaurs on
2. Hotfoot it to Londis for a tin of beans and a lucky dip.

Seas the Day

Chapter 2

'D'ya know, I've been on a diet for twenty-four years?' Trace Simkins complained as she and Sharon sat philosophising (moaning their tits off) over a frothy coffee and a sticky bun in Greggs.

Another non-perk to working in retail is that your days off are mostly always in the week when nothing's happening because everybody else is at work and school. Still, their mid-week, mid-morning powwows were the highlight of the week for Sharon. 'Really?' She asked her long-time friend and confidant under elevated brows, though she really wasn't surprised.

'Yeah. I worked it out the other day. Twenty-four years it's been.' Trace's heavily-kohled eyes surveyed the as-yet untouched pink iced bun on Sharon's plate. 'Er … you gonna eat that?'

She shook her head and pushed the plate across the table. 'So, how much weight have you lost in that time?'

'Not a pissing ounce!' Trace scoffed, mouth wide open, mangled iced bun doing laps inside. 'I'm bloody forty and it's gotten to the point that I just can't be arsed with it anymore, Shaz. I'm divorced. I'm Single. Bugger me! You've gotta 'ave some pleasure in life, ain'cha?'

Sharon poured a long sigh into her coffee cup; *Pleasure? what's that? Asking for me.*

Trace blinked back at her with narrowed eyes. 'You've a face as long as a kite. What's wrong?'

With a summons for council tax landing on the mat that morning, a boiler on the blink, a bathroom leak, Dawn in her hair, Stella under her skin and Gary always out on the piss, the question was more *what's right?* Still, if she didn't want to bore the arse off her only real friend with a long-winded account of all that was wrong in her life, then she needed to narrow it down a little. 'Stella's been giving Izzy Calpol again for no reason.'

Weirdly, Trace's face seemed to light up. 'She's a woman after my own heart!'

'Pardon?'

'I've been chuggin' that stuff since I was a nipper! Always keep a bottle handy, even now. The strawberry one. Godda be the strawberry one!'

Sharon's mouth fell agape. 'So, you're telling me that you, a childless woman in her forties, also has Calpol for no reason?'

'Sometimes.'

Sharon knew that her friend had a sweet tooth, but Christ! 'Trace, that's dangerous! Come on, they teach kids stuff like this in schools.'

'Well, I figured if babies have it, then a teaspoon

now and then ain't gonna hurt a heifer like me, is it?' she reasoned. 'Anyway, they shouldn't make it taste so nice, should they?'

'It's just to get fussy kids to swallow it, Trace. Not to tempt grown-arse adults!'

Trace threw her a look that said *Killjoy* and licked her sticky fingers clean. 'Anyway, what's Bitchface's game? What's she doling out the Calpol for?'

'Well, last time, she reckoned Izzy was *warm to the touch*,' Sharon recounted with a jaded eye roll, 'I said, *of course, she is! It's a warm day!*' Honestly, Trace, the woman's off her nut. I tried a cheaper washing powder the other week and it brought Izzy out in a rash. Stella wanted to take her to A&E! Said it might be Kawasaki disease.'

Trace frowned. 'Kawasaki … ain't that a motorbike?'

Sharon shrugged. 'Well, I'd never heard of it either, till she mentioned it. Honestly, she's like a walking encyclopaedia of medical conditions. I swear, Trace, illness to her is what Krispy Kreme doughnuts are to you.'

Trace blinked back at her, goggle-eyed. 'Are you telling me illness is the first thing she thinks about when she opens her eyes in the morning?'

'Bet your arse it is.'

Trace's gaze veered off toward the young woman in her twenties who was walking past the table at that moment and Sharon knew instinctively that the conversation was about to revert to her weight in around 0.3 seconds.

'D'ya know, I'd love to wear some of these nice jumpsuits what they're all wearing. All those pretty florals and pastels,' she mumbled, indignantly.

Sharon sank back into her chair. 'Then why don't you? They make pretty much everything in plus-size these days.'
From the look on Trace's face, you'd think she'd just been propositioned for sex by Scooby Doo. 'Listen, mate. Size eight to ten like you? Boooodiful! But a big bird like me? Pfft! Tubby toddler in a romper suit with a very full nappy springs to mind! It's like I've always said, *just because they do it in your size, don't mean you can wear it.*'

A sympathetic *hmm* was the best Sharon could offer. She was, after all, speaking to a self-confessed Calpol addict. They both knew she was beyond help.

A bleak silence ensued as Sharon's mind wandered back to her own troubles. 'Do you ever feel like you've come to a crossroads in life, Trace?'

'Eh?'

'A crossroads,' she repeated, 'you know, it's like you've arrived at a point in life where you're questioning everything: where you've been, where you're going, what's next.'

Trace shrugged. 'Dunno. You obviously have, though.' She tucked her funky, blue-black crop behind her ears with her bright pink talons and peered curiously across the table. 'Come on then, do tell.'

Sharon chewed her lip, cautiously cringing at the idea of letting loose the words that were lingering at the tip of her tongue. 'I'm unfulfilled.' *There!* She said it. And as the words left her mouth, they sounded even more pathetic out loud than she'd feared.

The dubious look Trace threw her confirmed her suspicions. 'How can *you* possibly be unfulfilled? You're married, you've got Izzy, you're thin! That's a full bingo card of my heart's desires!'

'The grass ain't always greener though, Trace. Trust me.'

'How'd you mean?'

'I mean, I thought I'd have made it by now. You know, been someone. Done way more than I have. I'm not where I want to be.'

Trace puffed out a long exhalation of breath. 'Is anyone, though? I'd like to be in Danny Dyer's underpants, but I ain't.'

She was right. Everybody wants more. But those who do fall into two camps:

Camp A: Talks about what they want at every given opportunity, does nothing about it, gives up, and falls straight back into position in the rat race.

Camp B: Talks about what they want at every given opportunity, tries various ways and means of getting it, doesn't give up, then eventually gets what they want. Sharon knew which she was in. 'I'm serious, Trace. I really want to change my life.'

'So, change it then,' she muttered, reaching for her coffee cup.

'I would, but I don't know where to start. I know what I think might make me happy, but I don't know how to get it.'

'Well, what is it you want?'

'I want my own business, Trace. I want to be a success,' Sharon told her in a hell-bent whisper.

'Doing what?'

She gave a downward glance. 'That's the thing, I don't know. But there's gotta be something we can make a living out of.'

Trace chuckled, placing her coffee cup down on the plate with a chink. 'Well, you can be anything you want in this town. Just ask the Puppet Man.'

True, thought Sharon. The Puppet Man had become a local legend for his unique street entertainment. He was living proof that anything is possible.

'Do you think Gary and I could really go into business with three GCSEs between us, though?'

Trace gave an ardent nod. 'Well, look at that Richard Branston fella. He left school with sod-all qualifications and just look at him now! He's got his name on pickle jars and tins of beans everywhere!'

Sharon wrinkled her nose. 'Um … it's Richard *Branson*, Trace. He's the owner and founder of Virgin.'

She gave an unruffled shrug. 'Potato, patata. The guy's filthy rich and he came from nothing, that's all yer need to know, innit?'

'Suppose.'

'Take it from me, Shaz. Richard Branston ain't got nothing you ain't got. There's only one thing what's got him to where he is today and it ain't privilege or intellect.' She leaned across the table with a sparky smile: 'it's pure drive.'

Sharon's face lit up. She had more drive than Toyota! Suddenly, there was hope on the horizon.

Usually, when Izzy asked to go to the arcades after school she was met with an emphatic *no*, but as Sharon witnessed kids everywhere scrambling off excitedly to their street dancing classes and football practice, she didn't have the heart. 'Okay, but just the penny falls, yeah?'

'Yessssss!' she beamed, fist-punching the air.

As they headed off hand-in-hand toward the seafront that balmy afternoon, Sharon had no idea that their spontaneous little jaunt was about to set the wheels of change in motion.

They were chatting away as she inadvertently spotted it: the *for-sale* sign outside an uninhabited white Victorian-style Bed and Breakfast. Though it was run down and looked about as fed up as Sharon felt, it had a certain je ne sais quoi. She gazed up at the hanging sign swaying cheerlessly in the sea breeze: 'Driftwood,' she muttered under her breath. It was perfectly positioned for business; slap-bang along the seafront in the thick of it all. All it needed was a good lick of paint and a chance. *Could be a nice little venture for someone,* Sharon thought to herself as they passed. She stopped and turned to look back again. Then once more.

'Could you ever see yourself running a B&B?' She asked Gary as he came to bed reeking of booze late that evening.

'Never thought about it,' he muttered, unzipping his flies and belching.

She hauled herself up on her elbows and turned to face him. 'Well, think about it now.'

His face fell momentarily straight. 'Right, I've thought about it and, *no*, I can't say that I could.'

'Why not?' She probed, tracing the edges of the worn embroidery on the duvet cover with her fingertips. 'What does anyone else who runs a B&B have that you don't?'

He turned and stared at her as though she'd gone stark raving mad. 'I don't know the slightest bloody thing about running a business!'

'Nor did Richard Branston … *Branson*,' she corrected herself. Jeez, now even she was saying it wrong. 'You do realise that Virgin got its name because Sir Richard and his partners were all new in business?'

'So?' he shrugged. 'Why are we even having this

conversation?'

'Just an idea … you know, for the future.' She felt her face crumple as, peevishly, he tore back the duvet, pausing momentarily as he caught sight of the see-through nightie she'd put on in a last-ditch attempt to ignite some passion. She flashed him a coquettish smile as he went to speak.

'You wanna be careful walking around in that thing,' he grunted, 'You can see yer boobs through it.'

Her mouth fell agape as he climbed into bed, turned his back on her and switched out the bedside lamp plunging them into darkness.

Friday night soon rolled around and, after the usual perfunctory peck on the doorstep, Gary left for Sheffield. Sharon noticed the sudden spring in his step as he strode out the front gate and, as she stood watching the car disappear off down the street, she remembered how he used to say that it was him and her against the world. These days, it was just her.

Most people spend their weeks holding out for the weekend. Nothing incentivises getting through the Monday-Friday slog more than the promise of lie-ins, lazy mornings, TV, and takeout. But as the tumultuous yattering of the seagulls alerted to the dawning of a drizzly Saturday morning that, as usual, she was down to work, Sharon was feeling far removed from *that weekend feeling*. Little did she know, it was about to get a whole lot worse.

She had showered and been putting on her bra when she felt it: a lump in her left breast. She froze, checking and checking again. No, she wasn't mistaken. It was there. *Oh my God!* She stood frozen to the spot; blood running cold.

Izzy was downstairs eating her Cocopops. The house was silent, a chamber of nothingness. Nobody was there to put an arm around her and tell her not to panic. That it was probably just nothing and to carry on with her day and make an appointment on Monday when the doctor's surgery opened. There was no voice of reason, just the stentorian one in her head telling her *this is it: game over.* She'd been so busy being unfulfilled that she'd forgotten the old adage: *health is wealth.* She'd been lost inside her own head for so long; estranged from reality. Now reality was banging the front door down, and, within minutes, she was outside her folk's two-bed terrace on Northgate Street doing the same.

Sharon's mother, Sue's, voice emanated from behind the glass as she scuffled with the chain. 'Listen, I do not wanna adopt a bleedin' Orangutan!' Her scowl softened as the door flew open to reveal Sharon and Izzy stood at the doorstep. 'Oh, It's you two. You're early.' By the time she had tightened the belt of her fluffy, blue

George at Asda dressing gown and taken a drag of her fag, her motherly sixth sense had kicked in already. 'Blimey, what is it? What's wrong?'

Sharon shook her head, unable to speak.

Sue's eyes darted, awkwardly. 'Er … come inside the both of you, yes, come in. But I'll just warn you…' She paused, looking cautiously toward the sitting-room door and lowered her voice to a covert whisper; 'Norma's round again.'

What, at 8.26 AM? Oh, my bloody life!

Norma, or *Nutty Norma* as she was affectionately known, lived alone a few doors down, and although some thought the widely used nickname she'd acquired unkind, others thought it merciful. It really all depended on whether you had the patience necessary to deal with her when she turned up on your doorstep wearing a swimming costume at three o'clock in the morning, or 'fainted' at your feet for attention. She'd pretend she was having a heart attack sometimes, too. One minute, she'd be enthusing about the middle aisle buys in Aldi over a cuppa and biccy, the next, she'd be wide-eyed, clutching her chest. You never knew what trickery she had up her sleeve or when it was coming. It was all for the fuss. She loved nothing more than an ambulance blue-lighting its way to her while some poor sod who really needed one had to wait even longer. She always had something to give you, too. Never anything decent, just old tat that was either fit for a skip or had come from one; like the car wing mirror she once gave Sharon to use as a make-up mirror. She was harmless enough, but she was, as Sharon's dad, Jim, had often said: *like a stray cat; let her in once and you're feckin' doomed!*

Sue, however, felt sorry for her, which made everybody *feckin' doomed* by default. *But she's lonely, Jim! Her boys never visit her*, she'd argue.

Aye, she's daft, but they're bloody not! He'd say.

Sharon teetered on the doorstep, steeling herself to walk into the house. Usually, she'd just go along with the facade. Sit and smile in polite exasperation while Norma told her that her daughter was pregnant (everyone knew she didn't have a daughter), that she'd had to have her dog put down (everyone knew she didn't have a dog) and that the new conservatory was coming along a treat (everyone knew she lived in a first-floor council-owned flat). She'd lost count of the number of times she'd had to put Norma into the recovery position for no reason, but today, she couldn't. She just couldn't. Her mind was consumed by her earlier discovery: *that thing* growing inside of her. 'Can't we just call an ambulance and be done with it? It'll be here in a few minutes, then we'll be rid of her,' she suggested in a low voice.

Sue looked appalled. 'No, Sharon! We can't do that; the NHS is on its bloody knees!'

'I've found a lump.'

'You, what?'

'A lump … in my breast'.

Sue fell silent and a look of worry etched its way across her face. 'Right. We'll just have to pretend we're going out. Yes. Yes, that's it, we're going out.' She pushed open the sitting-room door with a squeak which slowly gave way to reveal Norma lying on the floor, arms outstretched like Jesus on the cross. She was wearing a floral nightie and a bloody, great pink fascinator in her unkempt grey mane. Sue threw Sharon a look of dread. 'Right. You get one arm, I'll get the other, love.' Just as they moved to do so, Norma's eyes flew open.

Sue hovered over her. 'I'm ever so sorry, Norma, but we've got to dash.'

'Where we going?' She asked, a rictus, joker-like grin making its way up her face.

Sue closed her eyes and gave a jiggered sigh. 'Er ... well, it's just the three of us actually, Norma. We're ...' She looked to Sharon for support who blinked back at her, vacantly.

'Is the ambulance here, yet?' Norma asked.

'Oh, no, Norma. They're very busy. You'll just have to go home and put your feet up.'

'Oh, I ain't got time, Sue. I've got a wedding ter go to,' she replied with a gummy grin, smoothing down her nightdress.

Sue's eyes lit up. 'Oh, well you'd better hurry then, Norma. You don't want to be late to church!'

'Yes. I'd best me on me way.'

An awkward silence ensued when Norma did not get up from her reclined position on the carpet.

Suddenly, Sue snapped. She reached down, took

Norma by the elbow, and walked her to the front door. 'Come on then, Norma. I'll see you out. Shame you couldn't stay to chat for longer, but we've got somewhere we need to be.'

'That's alright, I'll come round when you're back'.

'NO!'

Norma's face fell.

'Well, you'll be at your wedding, won't you?' Sue reminded her.

'What wedding?'

Strewth! Sue slowly closed the door on her. 'Thanks for popping by, see you soon, Norma, byeee.'

'How on earth do you put up with that?' Sharon asked, once Norma had given up lamping the living shit out of the front door.

Sue let out a pent-up wail and clutched her chest. Norma was hard work. Just five minutes with her left Sue feeling like she needed a fortnight in a health spa. 'It's only now and then. She won't come in when your dad's here. He can't bloody stand her!'

'Where is he?'

'Where he always is, down the beach'.

As well as a hardy northerner, frugal zealot and all-round miserable git, Sharon's dad, Jim, was a thalassophile, a true lover of the sea. The ocean spoke to him in ways mere mortals couldn't. *All that sandy coastline reet on't doorstep*, he'd say, *there are folk who'd give their left bollock fer it*. When the weather was fine, he would plant himself on a bench along the promenade and spend hours just looking out to sea. Bearded scruff bag that he was – the pound shop version of his idol, Karl Marx – passers-by often mistook him for a tramp and would ambush him with all manner of hot drinks and snacks which he didn't mind at all.

'I dunno. The lengths we've to go to just to get some bloody peace around here,' Sue grunted, roughly drawing the blinds. She motioned toward the window. 'Norma sometimes looks in to see who's at home.'

'Does she?'

'Oh, aye! Nearly gave your dad a bleedin' heart attack a few weeks back. He was sat in the armchair reading his paper when she appeared at the glass in one of those celebrity masks, you know, the cardboard ones what they sell down Regent Road?'

'Really? Which one?'

'Prince Charles.'

Sharon barely managed a smirk.

Sensing her daughter's anguish, Sue fetched her purse from her handbag and fished out a two-pound coin. 'Here y'are, Izzy, pop to the newsagents and get yourself some sweets while me and your mum have a chat. Come through, Sharon, love. I'll stick the kettle on.'

They withdrew into the kitchen and Sue set about making the tea, a good old cuppa: the answer to everything.

'So, when did you find this lump?' Sue asked, filling the kettle over by the sink.

'Only this morning.'

'And what's Gary said about it?'

'He doesn't know. He's away in Sheffield.'

She spun around in fury. 'Not another pool tournament?'

Sharon's apathetic grunt confirmed it.

'I've never known someone to be away playing pool as much as your Gary. How on earth can you afford it?'

'We can't.'

Sue shook her head lethargically and slammed the kettle down to boil. 'And, how big is this lump?'

'I dunno. Maybe around the size of a penny.'

She nodded. 'Does it hurt?'

'No.'

After a wistful sigh, she drew in a preparatory breath. 'Well, let's see if we can get you seen at the walk-in.'

'I've got work at eleven,' Sharon reminded her, picturing Dawn crouched in wait behind a massive garden gnome.

Sue pulled her reading glasses down from atop her head, swiped her phone from the kitchen counter and stood tapping away at the screen. 'Well, give them a call and tell them you won't be in today. You can't work with this hanging over you.'

Sharon shook her head insistently. 'I was late this week. They won't take too kindly to me going off sick an' all.'

Sue emitted a loud, indignant sigh. 'I'll tell you something, these cut-throat firms forget they're dealing with real human beings. In an ideal world, nobody would ever run late or be ill but, hey, such is life! It's not like you can plan to find a lump in your breast on your day off.'

The sudden clamour of the back door opening took them both by surprise as Jim, who'd returned from his beach walk, cowered apprehensively behind it.

'You needn't worry yourself, she ain't here,' Sue told him in a vocal eye roll.

'Thank chuff for that!' He sighed, quickly straightening up and reclaiming his machismo. With a cursory glance in Sharon's direction, he pulled off his sandy Crocs and second-guessed the gloomy atmosphere. 'Don't tell me, he's spent all't housekeepin' down't boozer!'

Sharon stared at the fridge as Sue enlightened him and he stood giving his beard a contemplative stroke the way he always did during a crisis. A keen borrower (thief) of the motivational quotes of famous, historical figures, Jim was brimming with purloined pearls of wisdom. He'd know exactly what to say. He clicked his tongue. 'Well, there's no point crying about it till you've summat ter cry about, lass. Just get down't quacks, get the ball rolling and let's see what we're up against.'

It was hardly Karl Marx, but it was sound advice.

Sharon let out a deep sigh. It was such a kick in the teeth and so typical for fate to lay this on her now. Up to this morning, she'd been a woman on a mission to change her life. Could it really all be over before she'd even begun?

Rock the Boat

Chapter 3

James Paget Hospital, Gorleston.

The procession of cars slowly stalked the jam-packed car park like sharks, circling opportunistically, and pouncing all at once when a space opened up.

Gary shook his head, 'Madness. Bloody madness!'

'We're going to be late for the appointment,' Sharon fretted, gnawing at her nails which were already bitten down to the nub.

'Well, you get off and I'll catch you up,' he suggested, coolly.

'N-no … I can't face it by myself.'

Gary leaned across and opened the passenger door, failing to read the look on his wife's face that screamed *I need you!*

'Go on, out yer get. I'll catch you up as soon as I've parked,' he said, as though they might've been anywhere: a park, a restaurant, the DIY store.

Eyes welling, Sharon clicked open her seatbelt

and clambered out of the car. Today was D-day. She was about to get the results of her biopsy. It felt as though she was on her way to receiving the death penalty as she wandered toward the hospital entrance door. *When I come to walk out this door, I'll know my fate*, she thought as she drifted through it, unsure if finally having an answer would be a good thing. Her feet click-clacked along the shiny flooring on autopilot until they arrived at the correct department. In a mousey voice she didn't recognise, she checked in with the receptionist, then perched on a seat in the waiting area where her eyes remained glued to the doorway. *He'll be here any minute.*

A smartly dressed older woman walked in and took a seat opposite. Her fully made-up face looked equally as fraught as Sharon's. Her eyes were distant, mouth tense. She cleared her throat continuously.

A few moments on, there came the sound of a door squeak followed by the formal voice she'd been dreading: 'Sharon Blewitt?'. She made one last hopeful glance toward the waiting room entrance, hoping with every fibre of her being that Gary would lumber through it that very second. He didn't. She took a deep breath and rose from her chair. *Here we go, this is it.*

'Take a seat,' said the consultant, waving toward the two chairs positioned opposite his own. His gaze flicked to the door and back. 'Do you have anyone with you today, Sharon?'

'My husband ... he's parking the car,' she managed. *Oh, shit! It's bad news! He's making sure I've got someone to drive me home once he's dropped the bombshell!* A wave of nausea came over her.

'Would you like to wait for him?'

'N-no, let's just carry on without him.'

'Are you sure? It's really no trouble.'

It's bad news. I know it! 'Yes, I'm sure. Go ahead.' As her pulse did the Salsa, Sharon watched the consultant open a file and take out an X-ray picture. He needn't have bothered pointing out the mass. It was the first thing she saw.

'Okay, let's cut to the chase,' he began as she braced herself for the words she felt sure were coming. 'Sharon, you have what we call a Fibroadenoma.'

'A, w-what?'

'A Fibroadenoma,' he repeated. 'It's basically a benign lump. Very common. They often go away on their own, so we'll take a wait-and-see approach; give you regular scans.'

'Y-you mean, it's not cancer?'

He shook his head. 'No, definitely not.'

Sharon felt her entire body slump in relief as she took in the magnitude of those words: she wasn't dying. She still had the rest of her life in front of her. Another chance!

'Oh, thank God, thank God!' She repeated it over and over. 'Sorry, I must sound like a broken record.'

The consultant flashed a broad smile. This was the part of his job that he enjoyed most. 'Don't be.

It's excellent news. I'm sure it's come as a great relief to you.'

Gary still hadn't caught up by the time Sharon had reached the hospital entrance door. She closed her eyes in relief on the way out, thanking her lucky stars that this was to be the last of her recent visits to Stella's favourite hangout. Spotting him outside in the carpark, pacing up and down on his phone, Sharon frowned. *What's he doing?* She caught the tail end of his conversation on approach. 'Look, I'll let you know as soon as! I've gotta go.' His voice was tense. He looked up, ended the call, and stuffed his phone into his trouser pocket. 'Sorry, baby. That was work wanting to know when I'll be in. Did you get your results, then?'

'Yeah.'

'And…?'

'It's benign.'

'Be-what?'

She felt the last dregs of her patience drain away. 'It's not bloody cancer, alright?!'

'See? What did I say? Told yer it'd be nothing,' he chuckled, dismissively. 'I'll just go and pay the ticket. Car's parked over there next to that silver Beemer.'

Sharon watched him stride off, whistling away as though he hadn't a care in the world.

A few minutes later, he returned to the car, and they drove away in silence. They do say that silence is golden, but in the Blewitts' case at this moment in time, it only amplified everything annoying about Gary – everything from his whistle to the sniff he seemed to make every ten seconds; even the way he changed gear was annoying. Just lately, everything he did seemed to get on his wife's tits, and she didn't like the irritable person she became in his company.

He seemed to sense the tension that hung in the air like a bad fart, and gave her a cursory glance as he took a left. 'Well, you don't look very chuffed for someone who's just been given a clean bill of health.'

She couldn't hide her frustration any longer. 'Why did you take so long to park?'

He huffed, indignantly. 'Did it escape yer notice how busy the place was?'

Suddenly, she erupted like Mount Etna. 'You weren't there, Gary. You're never bloody there!'

He frowned toward her, 'yes, I am! I'm here now, aren't I?'

'Now it's all over, you mean!'

His look of resentment was no match for hers. 'I've been terrified, Gary! How could you not realise that?'

'Well, you had nuffin' ter be terrified about. I've been telling yer that all along.'

'And how could you possibly have known that for a fact? Because as far as I was concerned, I was about to get a death sentence!'

He paused for a moment. 'Yeah, but yer didn't,

did yer?' And that was it: the final nail.

'Just take me home and get off back to work, I've had enough!' She wasn't lying.

Squashing down the contents of the tatty suitcase which she'd nearly broken her neck fetching down from the attic, Sharon yanked the tarnished zip full circle and gave it an accomplished pat. 'Well, that's one way to get out of cleaning the oven.'

Day-off afternoons were usually reserved for housework, but not today. Sharon and Izzy were leaving. She didn't know where they were going, just that they were leaving.

As she lumped the case down the stairs and set it down beside the front door, she was hit by a tidal wave of doubt. Gary was all she'd ever known. They'd spent half their lives together. He knew every part of her: the fighter and the frightened, the strong and the sensitive, the dreamer and the doubter, the helper and the helpless. Their union had not been "The Notebook," not by any bloody means, but it was familiar. Going it alone was a scary prospect after all this time. Still, there's nothing like a health scare to make you take stock. She'd just been given a new lease of life and she needed to live it. If not now, *when?*

Her stomach turned over as Gary walked

through the door a little after five that evening – well, not really *walked*, more ploughed straight into the suitcase that was ready to go by the door. A brief struggle followed as he grappled to keep his balance. 'What the... what's all this?'

She moped into the hallway with folded arms and took a deep breath. 'I'm leaving you, Gary.'

'You, what?'

'You heard me.'

He did that patronising half-laugh he always did whenever she was trying to be serious. 'What are you talking about, yer doughnut? Leaving me? What for?!'

She stared at him incredulously. 'I think we both know that you and I are on different paths. We want different things. We've drifted apart.'

He went all stiff. 'Don't ... don't you want me?'

Christ, he sounds like a Human League record! Sharon bit her lip and said nothing until, weirdly, he started chuckling. 'Erm ... how is this in any way funny, Gary?!'

He nervously ran a hand through his greying crew cut and puffed out a long exhalation of breath. 'I've just bought a B&B.'

She made a face. 'Sorry?!'

'I've bought us a B&B along the seafront. Our own business. Just like you wanted.'

She released a dubious sigh. 'Gary, we've got bills coming out of our arses. Sometimes we can't even *wipe* our arses! And you're telling me you've bought a B&B?'

He nodded, insistently. 'Just exchanged contracts.'

'And how did you pay for it? Magic bloody beans?!'

'I've put down half as a deposit and taken out a commercial mortgage on the rest.'

She stared back at him in disbelief. 'You're off your rocker. We're skint!'

He shook his head. 'No, we ain't. Not anymore.' An addled silence ensued. 'Alright, cards on the table,' he said, dropping his arms to his side. It's all been happening in the background for some time. If I've seemed preoccupied lately, well, that's one reason why. I've had a lot going on and I had ter keep it all hush-hush 'cos it was meant ter be a big surprise. I wasn't gonna tell you nuffin about it till I was holding the keys in me hands. Then you had your health scare and … well, I know I like ter put a brave face on things, but I hadn't planned for something like that to happen. I've been scared, too.'

The beginnings of a smile flickered on Sharon's lips. So he did care, after all.

'Anyway, none of that matters now,' he said with a dismissive wave of the hand. He lunged forward and grabbed her by the shoulders. 'We've come into some money, baby!'

'You what?'

'I've inherited a third of me Uncle Ted's estate.'

'Uncle, who?'

'Uncle Ted! On me dad's side.'

Sharon raised a brow.

'He's proper minted. Lived in Dubai since I was a nipper. I've definitely mentioned him over the years. Don't you remember?'

She shook her head. Maybe he had, but it didn't ring a bell. Still, he'd been estranged from his dad's side of his family since he was a lad, there was every chance he had family abroad.

'Well, anyway,' he continued, 'he's left behind a small fortune and there was only Dad, Auntie Jan and me named in the will. Uncle Ted never married, see? He had plenty of birds, but—'

'How much?' Sharon cut in.

He grinned intently, squeezing her hands. 'Enough to pay off our debts, start our own business and have a whole new life, Shaz. A fresh start!'

'How much?' She repeated.

'Half a million,' he muttered, quietly.

Sharon's mouth fell agape. *Fuck me, sideways!*

'When I found out how much I was getting, I knew exactly what to do with it,' he beamed. 'You were always saying you wanna be your own boss, run yer own business and live in a big gaff by the sea, well, this place has ten bedrooms and if it were any closer to the sea, it'd be in the bugger! Will that do for yer?'

Sharon stood with folded arms, taking it all in as he continued selling her the dream. 'We'll stick this dump on the market and leave our jobs. Be our own bosses!' He wheedled.

OMG. No more bloody Dawn! Her growing smile dropped suddenly. 'But you said that you don't know the first thing about running a business,' she pointed out, recalling the night she'd worn the see-through nightie, which had been as pointless as when people stick their hands out for a bus that's going to stop anyway … then continue holding it out right up to the moment it grinds to a complete halt beside them.

Gary gave a wry chuckle. 'I know what I'm doing with the business side of things, baby. I've taken proper advice. I'm having a business plan drawn up, costing, the lot! I was just saying that ter throw you off the scent. When you suddenly mentioned running a B&B, I thought you'd gone and bloody found out, somehow.'

She stared at him quizzically. 'This isn't one of your daft jokes, is it?'

He rolled his eyes to the ceiling. 'When have I ever joked about something like this?'

True. 'So, how come I've never seen any letters through the post about the sale?'

Gary didn't hesitate. 'I know this accountant fella, Rob. I play pool with him, sometimes. Well anyway, he's been helping me out. All the paperwork's gone through his office, you know, ter help keep it on the downlow.'

'And the inheritance?'

'Auntie Jan was named executor of the will and she didn't have our address, so she tracked me down on Facebook last year and gave me the news.

I met her at the solicitors down the quay to sign everything once the probate process was finalised, then I hid the cheque when it arrived.'

'But there's sod all in the bank!' Sharon protested. In fact, there had only been four quid in it last time she checked.

Gary shook his head. 'That's because it went into another account, baby. A new one I opened so that you wouldn't see the money when it cleared a few weeks back.' He must've sensed that she wasn't convinced. 'Look! See for yerself!' He said, tapping away on his phone before turning the screen toward her.

Not accustomed to seeing so many digits in an available balance, Sharon very nearly wet herself. 'Bloody Nora!'

He gave a self-congratulatory nod. 'That's what's left after the deposit and a few expenses,' he said, following as she tottered on jelly legs into the front room, collapsing onto the sofa in a daze.

'Listen, I know things have been shit, Shaz. But we've got all the ingredients to make it good, now. This is gonna be like another life for us … our own business! Holidays! Family time! Couple time! We ain't gotta worry about money no more! We can just fall in love all over again with no stress and nothing getting in the way this time. It'll just be you, me, and Izzy.' It was everything she'd been longing for. Everything she'd ever wanted. He crouched before her and stroked her knee. 'Look, we've only drifted apart because of circumstance.

If we can't make it with all this, then fair enough. But we'll never know unless we give it a try. Let's at least give it one more go, yeah? Hmm?'

He trailed soft, slow kisses down her neck as she sat staring into space.

'Show me it. I want to see it,' she murmured.

'Alright,' he muttered, moving to undo his belt.

She slapped his arm in horror. 'Not that! I meant the B&B!'

He took his phone out of his pocket, then paused. 'The estate agents have probably taken the listing down from the website by now. It's been a couple of weeks since the sale went through.'

'Well, at least have a look and see.'

He began tapping and scrolling on his phone. 'Nah, they've taken it down. Thought they would've.'

'Well, where about is it?'

'Along the seafront.'

Her face lit up. There was only one B&B Sharon knew of that had been up for sale along the seafront. 'Can't you show me a single picture of it?'

'I can do better than that, baby. I'll take yer to see it in person.'

She picked at her cuticles as the million-dollar question burned. 'Do you love me, Gary?'

'You, what?'

'It's just that you don't seem to say it much these days.'

He scratched his head and frowned back at her. 'Well, I don't feel the need to. You know I love you.

All of me loves all of you.'

'Can't you ever be serious?' She sighed.

He huffed, indignantly. 'I am being serious.'

'No, you're not. You're borrowing from song lyrics, again.'

'I was not!'

'Yes, you were. That was John bloody Legend!'

He shrugged, indifferently. 'I mean it though, Shaz. I do, honestly. C'mon, whaddya say? Let's not throw away twenty years together. We owe it to ourselves to try. If not for our sake, then let's do it for Izzy.'

Sharon stared at the worn arm of the sofa, quietly weighing up the alternative: starting life all over again as a single mum past her prime with no savings, no career, and no fixed abode. She didn't have to think about it for very long. 'Okay … let's try again.'

Gary lunged forward, hoisted her off the sofa and twirled her around in the air as though he'd just won the lottery. 'You know it makes sense, baby! It's gunna be amazing, I promise!'

'Dah! Alright! Put me down you wolly!'

'Listen, go and get yer glad rags on, yeah? Now the cat's out the bag, we might as well go out and celebrate.'

'Glad rags?' Sharon parroted. 'I don't know if I've got anything in my wardrobe that'll pass for that.' *Sad rags* was more like it.

Gary reached into his trouser pocket and took out his wallet which was notably fatter looking. He flipped it open, slid out a bundle of crisp notes and thrust them into her hand. 'Here y'are. Nip out to the retail park and get something. Treat yourself!'

Sharon jokingly held the wad of cash up to the light.

'Cheeky bugger, I'll have it back if yer don't want it!' He laughed and threw it up into the air, then pulled her down onto the tatty carpet where, in a frenzy of squeals and giggles, they kissed like it was 1999.

The sun was still out in force in the early evening sky and the seafront was heaving. Sharon's brand-new maxi dress rippled in the sea breeze as she and Gary held hands for the first time in ages, while Izzy walked on ahead. If the smiles they exchanged could speak, they'd have said *if you're happy and you know it, clap your hands.*

'Where did you say you'd booked, again, Gaz?'

'Chiccos. Supposed to be pukka!'

It was crazy that they'd lived locally all this time, and yet, could count on one hand the places they'd tried of the plethora of places to eat in town.

'Hey, Dad, now that you're loaded, can I get an iPad? I mean, a proper one. The real thing,' Izzy asked, tugging the sleeve of his shirt as they climbed the steps and entered the restaurant to the ambrosial tang of steak and seafood.

'Course, yer can! The very latest model.'

'Oh my God, yesssss!'

Gary ordered champagne and pored over the menu as they sat down at the table. 'Cor, we're gonna eat alright tonight, baby. Look at this lot!'

When the drinks arrived, he picked up his glass and raised it up in a toast. 'To the future!' He grinned, 'Oh, and ter Bernard Matthews, who just lost his best customer. From now on, he can bloody well shove his Turkey Dinosaurs up his arse!'

'I'm not sure he's even alive anymore, Gaz,' Sharon giggled.

'Is he not?'

'Don't think so.'

He shrugged and they clinked glasses. She genuinely could not remember the last time she'd felt this happy.

'Mum, which one do I use?' Izzy whispered, motioning toward the cutlery as, a little later on, the starters arrived at the table in a veil of appetising steam.

Sharon paused to think about it for a moment. 'Um...'

'Here y'are, look. This is yer salad fork, that's yer soup spoon, here's yer dinner fork, that's yer dinner knife, this is yer dessert spoon and that's yer butter knife,' Gary cut in, in one sprinting breath.

Sharon threw him an applauding look. 'Get you!' Turning her attention to her king prawn starter, she stabbed one with her fork, held it under her nose and examined it, warily. 'They'll be a bit … crunchy, won't they?'

Gary looked up from his plate and laughed. 'Nah. You've gotta remove the head and tail first, baby,' he enlightened her, going on to demonstrate with the skill of a chef.

'Excuse me, but how do you suddenly know so much about food?' She demanded, playfully.

He gave a modest shrug. 'Ainsley Harriott.'

'Shall we have some more champagne?' Sharon asked, nodding toward her empty glass as the evening drew on.

'Go steady, baby. You don't want a hangover, you've got work in the morning,' Gary cautioned, sliding his spoon through his mountainous ice cream sundae.

She responded with a slight snigger. 'You seriously don't think I'm going into work tomorrow when we've got all that dough in the bank, do you?'

He paused; his spoon suspended in mid-air. 'Baby, that money's not for us to live off. Tonight's just a celebratory treat.'

She blinked back at him.

'We need it for all the set-up costs,' he explained, noticing her perplexity. 'It's gunna cost a pretty penny ter get the place up to scratch and kitted out before we can open. You can't just jack yer job in, now. You'll have ter wait. At least until it's all gone through, and we've got the keys.'

He was right. Of course, he was.

'How long till then?'

'Dunno. It'll take as long as it takes, won't it?' Sharon released a wistful sigh across the table which wasn't wasted on Gary. 'Look, it won't be long, baby. I promise. Just hang on in there.'

'Heyyy, I wanna go see the B&B! Let's walk past it,' Sharon slurred as they doddered out the restaurant door in food comas into the night-time, technicolour razzmatazz outside.

Gary didn't seem quite so enthusiastic. 'Nah, the place is in darkness, innit? I'll take you's both down at the weekend, then yer can have a proper look in the daylight, yeah?' He pulled her into him. 'Besides, I wanna get you home. We've got a lotta lost ground ter make up for,' he mumbled into her hair, sending a tingle of lust careering down her spine. It had been a long time.

Although the earth didn't move and Gary kept his socks on, Sharon felt the reconnection as the celebrations continued between the sheets. And, as they dozed off in each other's arms just like the old days, she slept properly for the first time in months.

Turn the Tide

Chapter 4

'Here y'are, this is it,' Gary announced, pulling into a cramped space along the seafront late on Saturday afternoon.

Sharon peered eagerly out the passenger window of their battered old Ford Focus and did a little jig as they drew up alongside it: the very same B&B she and Izzy had walked past weeks ago.

An excited gasp came from the back seat. 'Are we gonna live here?'

'Yeah, you like it, Iz?'

'It's so cool, Dad! I love it!'

The smell of doughnuts, candy floss and horse manure intermingled with the salty breath of the sea permeated the air as they stepped out onto the still-sunny pavement.

'The *for-sale* sign's still up!' Sharon frowned.

'You, what?' Gary spotted it and rolled his eyes. 'Gawd, I dunno. Lazy buggers them estate agents.' She watched as he marched toward it, pulled it out of the ground and slung it into a skip along the side street. 'Whaddya think, baby?'

'I love it!' She squeaked, excitedly. 'It's so quaint and—' She spun around and admired the bustling Golden Mile behind, the chaotic din of the arcade machines and the horse-drawn carriages clip-clopping past. 'Look at it! Smack bang in the middle of all the action. You couldn't want for a better position!'

'Yep!' Gary grinned, draping an arm around her shoulders. 'This is it now, Shaz. The eagle's landed!'

She nestled her head into his shoulder as they admired their exciting new venture. 'So, when do you reckon we'll get the keys? I'm dying for a look inside.'

'Any day now, baby,' he said, lowering his arm to her waist and pulling her closer. 'Pretty soon you'll have everything you ever wanted.'

Six weeks on, when they still didn't have the keys to the B&B, Sharon noted that the eagle hadn't landed at all. In fact, she was starting to wonder if the bugger had been shot on the way down! From errors on paperwork to the solicitors being short-staffed, there seemed to be setbacks at every turn and every day of delay meant another day working under Dawn bloody Turner! Knowing that she was within spitting distance of being her own boss was more of a frustration than a comfort. It was the weirdest feeling having this good fortune and, by the same token, nothing to show for it. Little had changed. The bills were still landing on the doormat and spilling out of the kitchen drawer.

Life was much the same as it had always been.

'I'm worried it's gonna fall through, Trace,' Sharon fretted during another tête-à-tête in Greggs, her knuckles white as she clutched her coffee cup. 'I've got so many ideas for the place. I've already decided on a Gatsby theme. Lots of little extras, the personal touch, you know? I want it to have a real boutique feel.'

'Sounds fab.'

'I just wish I knew why it was taking so long.'

'Property takes ages to sort, Shaz. It's these greedy solicitor firms. They take on more business than they can handle.'

'You think so?'

'Oh, totally!'

She gave a yearning sigh. 'I just wish it'd all hurry up. We've got all this money but Gary's refusing to touch a penny of it until the sale's gone through and a cost report's been drawn up for the refurbishment.'

'But that's only sensible, surely?' Trace reasoned, taking a bite of her still-too-hot sausage roll, which landed back upon its plate with a thud and the F-word.

Sharon bit her lip. 'Yeah, but I just … I dunno. Something's off. I don't know what it is. I don't feel properly on board with all this. It's as though it's his ship and he's steering it all by himself. I have to push him for updates constantly.'

'So, what are you saying?'

'Hm. I dunno. Maybe I'm just too impatient.'

'I was then gunna say the same thing, Shaz. What yer stressin' for? It's all come up roses for yer! You've got a clean bill of health and everything to play for. All you've gotta do is sit back and wait, now.'

'You're right. You're absolutely right. Anyway, here I am droning on and on about myself again. I'm turning into my sodding mother-in-law! How did your Tinder date go?'

'Don't bloody ask!'

'That bad, was it?'

Trace drew in a precursory breath. 'Well, I spent a hundred quid on some new shoes for the date: Steve Maddens, four-inch heel, silver. Boodiful! Anyway, I didn't know where he was taking me. I'd told him to just surprise me. Well, he only went and took me bowling, didn't he? So, I had to trade me Steve Maddens for them daft bloody bowling shoes. Anyway, cut a long story short, he was a right boring bastard. No conversation, whatsoever. So I got pissed, went home in the bowling shoes and now some shit's got me Steve Maddens!'

Sharon's eyes widened. 'How d'ya know?'

'Called 'em first thing Sunday morning. They said there weren't no shoes left behind matching that description, quelle bloody surprise!'

'Oh, Trace.'

'Tell me about it. I got about half hour's wear outta the buggers!'

Sharon gave her a commiserative pout. 'Aww. I

really thought you might get somewhere with this one. He looked nice.'

'I know, he was the first match I'd had in ages. Don't get me wrong, he weren't no Danny Dyer. I swiped him mainly 'cos he was the only one with his face fully in the picture, he didn't look like he was about ter punch someone, he weren't posing with a loada birds on his arm, and he weren't squatting down, holding some fuck-off great fish! Why do they do that? Why can't they just take a nice head and shoulders shot of themselves smiling nicely?'

'Beats me.' Sharon wasn't up to speed with all this online dating, and by the sounds of it, she should be thankful.

Trace took an angry bite of her now sufficiently cooled sausage roll. 'D'ya know, they weren't lying when they said the path to true love never runs smooth. I reckon some bugger's bulldozed mine!'

Though it hadn't worked out with her ex-husband, Colin, a dentist who was *boring as fuck*, Trace hadn't done too badly out of it. He'd allowed her to keep the house, a four-bed detached place on Windsor Avenue which they'd owned outright, and she'd enjoyed a tidy settlement which allowed her to be a lady of leisure. The *leisure* part was right enough, but Trace was no lady, and she'd never pretended to be. Her sad panda-like expression seemed to lift suddenly. 'Ooh! Now, that's what I meant to tell you!' She reached down to the side of her chair and brought her garish snakeskin-effect handbag up onto the table. Sharon watched in anticipation as she pulled her black Gucci glasses down from atop her head, fished out a business card from her purse and slid it across the table.

'Madame Catharina Psychic Fortune Teller' Sharon read aloud. 'What's this?'

'It's the new fortune teller what's opened down Regent Road.'

'Oh?'

'Yeah, me neighbour, Sandra, gave it me. She's had her fortune done. Reckons it's the biz. Proper accurate. Shall we pop down and get ours done?' Trace made it sound as normal and everyday a thing as getting a new set of nails.

Sharon pulled a face. 'What? No way! I'm not paying some charlatan to sit and tell me a load of mumbo-jumbo. I get enough of that when Gary comes home pissed from the pub.'

Trace's face fell. 'Oh. I thought they might be able to tell you about your future business success and me about me love life … or lack of.'

Sharon slid the card back across the table. 'Nah, there's someone out there for everyone, Trace. You don't need no fortune teller. You'll find him soon enough.'

'I better had. Honestly, I'm beginning ter forget what a fella's pecker looks like!'

Sharon observed the adjacent table of pensioners' heads shoot up in disgust while Trace sipped her coffee, bold as brass. 'And how's things going with your Gary in the bedroom department, these days?'

'We're back to once a week again,' Sharon divulged in a low voice with a slightly smug waggle of her brows.

'Once a week?! Me and my Colin used to do it most days. Toys, dress-up, the lot!' She trumpeted to all of Greggs, earning herself a roomful of eye rolls.

'Really? So where did it all go wrong for you's both?'

Her cerise-pink lips curled in contempt. 'Well, one thrust and it was all over. That's why we were always doing it! I know yer shouldn't base a relationship on sex, but I love it, Shaz. I do. And I keep tellin' yer, I need a proper alpha male who'll shag me from one end of the room to the other.'

She might as well have screamed it with a megaphone from the top of Nelson's monument, Sharon thought, wishing the ground would swallow her up as the entire cafe seemed to grind to a standstill. 'Um … er … shall we go and check out this fortune teller, then?'

'So, do you reckon this Madame Catheter's any good?' Sharon asked as they weaved through the crowds along Regent Road; the smell of fish and chips permeating the air.

'*Catharina!*' Trace corrected with an eye roll.

'Potato, patata!' Sharon quipped with a smirk

'Here y'are, I reckon this is it,' Trace announced as they approached a pillar-box-red painted shop front about halfway down. Both peered up in tandem at the shop sign, upon which, *Madame Catharina Psychic Fortune Teller* was emblazoned in bold, gold lettering.

'You go first,' Trace prompted, thumbing toward the entrance door.

'Sod off!'

'Oh, go on!'

'No. This was your bloody idea!'

She squinted her eyes back toward the door. 'It looks all dark and dingy. Could be anything going on behind those curtains.'

'Like what?! Look, just get inside before I change my mind.'

'Alright, alright!'

A wind chime jangled as Trace pushed open the door and cowered behind it, half expecting to have walked in on some sort of candle-lit sacrifice. Her face softened as she observed that, with its little waiting area, counter, and glass cabinets in which rows of crystals and decks of tarot cards were displayed for sale, it was much like any other shop.

'Get in, for God's sake!' Sharon giggled, shoving her into the door which knocked the wind chime down onto the polished wooden floor with a reverberating metallic clang. 'Oops!'

An invisible cloak of frankincense hung in the air and spiritual music tinkled away in the background. But there was no sign of Madame Catharina. Perhaps she'd appear in a puff of smoke.

They both spotted the sign by the counter

which read *all readings £30 payable upfront. Cash only*. Trace nodded toward it. 'She wants paying upfront.'

'Upfront? What if she's crap?'

There was no time for debate when, just then, a human-shaped mass they assumed was Madame Catharina, appeared through the beaded door curtain at the back of the shop. There was a brief struggle as she became entangled in it.

'Need a hand, love?' Trace called out to her, evoking a snort from Sharon who turned her back and began picking up and examining all manner of spiritual objects by means of a distraction.

'No, no. I am fine. It is zis stupid door curtain. It has gotten caught in my eawwings. I vill be vith you in a second.'

Eventually, she worked her way free and arrived at the counter in a flurry of floaty chiffon. She wore a purple beaded head scarf tied at one side and had the most soulful eyes; absolutely piercing blue they were, and deep, like a lagoon. 'Vhat can I do for you ladies?'

'We'd like our fortunes done, please,' said Trace, fishing her purse out from her bag.

'Vonderful. That'll be tirty pounds each.'

'Here y'are, I'll get yours, Shaz,' Trace chirped, sliding three, crisp £20 notes out from her purse and handing them to Madame Catharina who snatched them up like a greedy seagull and thrust them down her top, into her bra.

Sharon smiled gratefully.

'Okaaaay, my beautiful soul sisters, follow me around ze back,' Madame Catharina directed in a smoky voice. She was careful to hold the beaded door curtain to the side this time as they passed through it into a small room cloaked with red velvet curtains. A round table covered with a shimmery gold tablecloth and three chairs was positioned centre-space.

Sharon wondered if the weirdly wonderful Madame Catharina had been expecting them, somehow. *Nah, of course not. Nobody does this sort of thing without dragging a pal along. It's not in the slightest bit spooky that there are three chairs ready and waiting.*

'Vich of you vould like to go first?'

Both nominated each other with a firm point.

'A-ha-ha-ha, shall ve toss a coin?'

'Alright, I'll go first,' Trace relented. 'Where'd yer want me?'

'Just be seated and make yourselves comfortable whilst I light ze candles and tune in.'

Trace shuffled uncomfortably in her seat as they waited. 'I hope she don't light many more of those bleedin' candles. If one falls over, the whole place is likely to go up!'

'Sshhh!'

'Okaaaay, soul sister,' Madame Catharina trilled, placing a deck of shiny, silver tarot cards and a selection of crystals down onto the table. 'I am going to cut ze deck into four piles and place a crystal on top of each. Zhen, I vould like you to pick ze pile and ze crystal you are most drawn to, okay?'

'Okay.'

They watched, entranced, as she shuffled the cards with perfectly manicured, slender hands.

Sharon glanced down at her own bitten-down stumps and quickly tucked them away out of sight.

'Vell? Vhich is it to be?'

'Hm. That pink'un, there,' Trace decided. 'I love me pink.'

'Ahhh, yes. Ze Rose Quartz.' Madame Catharina pushed the other cards to the side of the table and picked up Trace's chosen pile. 'Now, zhen. Let's begin your reading.' She placed each card face-down on the table, threw her head back and closed her eyes.

Sharon wondered if she was about to do a 'Meg Ryan' in "When Harry Met Sally."

'Okaaay, I am tuned in and connected with source,' she announced as she began turning the cards over with a series of enlightened gasps and grunts.

'I see zhat you struggle wiz your weight,' she announced.

Sharon rolled her eyes. Christ, any bugger could see that!

'Your spirit guides are telling you to enjoy yourself. Life is too short to vorry about zhese things. You must love ze person zhat you are and vonce you do zhat, ozthers vill love you, too.'

She's got that from *Chicken Soup for the Soul!* Sharon thought.

'I can see zhat you are going to meet a man very soon and it vill be a verrry passionate love affair.'

Trace's head shot up like a rampant dog's. 'When?!'

'Source is telling me in ze next one, maybe two months.'

'Well, is there any way source can … you know, speed things up a bit? I'm a desperate woman!'

'A-ha-ha-ha. No, my dear. What is meant to be, vill be.'

'Bugger.'

'I can see zhat he is tall, dark, and handsome … in his own way. You are going to be verrry happy togezher. You vill not be able to keep your hands off each other. Like two randy teenagers, you know?'

Trace's eyes lit up. 'Any idea on this fella's name? Just so I can keep me eye out for him on Tinder.'

Madame Catharina stared long and hard at the cards. 'Hm. I am getting *Barry*.'

'Barry?!' Trace parroted, open-mouthed. 'He sounds old … old and bald. I can sense it.'

'Maybeee … *Larry*, even.'

'Larry?! Christ, that's even bloody worse! Goin' off yer description, I was thinking more along the lines of Carlos, or Enrique, or summin.'

Madame Catharina threw her a look that suggested she might be aiming a little too high.

'Just know that everyzhing zhat is on its way for you is meant for you. You are entering a vondferful phase in your life. I see travel, I see good times ahead, but you must also look after yourself and slow down a little.'

Ah, yes. The Standard psychic's spiel. Now all that's left to say is *you're psychic yourself*, thought Sharon.

'I also see zhat you are psychic yourself!'

Boom!

The icing on the cake came during Sharon's reading when Madame Catharina told her she was seeing another tall, dark, handsome man for her and that she was hearing *vedding bells* within the next one to two years. They'd heard it all, now.

'That neighbour of yours must be gullible as a fish. Christ, what a swizz!' Sharon fumed as they closed the shop door and ventured back out onto the street feeling thoroughly conned.

'Tell me about it! I'm debating going back inside to wrestle her for me sixty nicker back!'

Seeing that the post had arrived on what was another scorching Saturday morning, Sharon bent down and grabbed it on the way past. 'Oh, there's one for P. Goddard, whoever that is,' she muttered, combing out her wet hair as she wafted into the kitchen. 'Looks official.' She turned it over and back again. 'Might as well open it.'

Gary sprung up from the breakfast table with

half a crumpet hanging out his gob and snatched it from her hands. 'Give it here! You can't just open other people's mail, it's bloody illegal!' He fumed, raining specks of crumpet down about the place.

'Is it?'

'Yeah! Didn't no-one ever tell you that?'

She gave an indifferent shrug. 'Well, what else are we supposed to do with it? We don't know any *P. Goddard*.'

Gary grabbed a pen from the odds-and-sods drawer and began scribbling on the front of the envelope. 'You're supposed ter post it back, ain'cha?'

Sharon peered over his shoulder just about making out *not at this address* through the scrawl. 'Well, give us it here, I'll post it on the way to work.'

'Nah, I'll do it. You ain't got time, you're running late,' he said, folding and sliding it into the back pocket of his jeans.

'No, I ain't?!'

He kicked the kitchen door closed, yanked her toward him by the belt of her dressing gown and untied it with one hand, smirking devilishly as it dropped to the floor leaving her standing starkers before him. 'You are, now.'

'Ah, good evening, Sharon. Nice of you to join us,' came Dawn's latest attempt at sarcasm during another frantic dash up the escalator.

Keep it together, it's not for much longer. Keep it

together, it's not for much longer. The phrase had become a self-help mantra as the long wait for resignation day continued. It was easier said than done, though. Particularly when everywhere she looked, constant reminders of the dire need to quit came in the form of Dawn's bossy notes which seemed to pop up wherever she went:

In the staff fridge: *Please STOP using my Alpro oat milk! It clearly has my name written on it! Last time I checked, there was only one Dawn Turner on the payroll! This is THEFT! BUY YOU'RE OWN!!!*

In the staff room: *FYI, please STOP leaving empty wrappers behind! We have provided a bin pacifically for you're use! Kindly USE it!!!*

In the toilets: *Will the phantom bogey-wiper please STOP! This is NOT kindergarden! If you must pick you're nose, please use a tissue and then dispose of it!!!*

By the tills: *FYI, please finish till rolls COMPLETELY before replacing with new ones! The rainforests are dyeing!!!*

Sharon was tempted to go around all of them with a red pen, correct the spelling and grammar and write *please see me* at the bottom. *Perhaps I'll do it on my last day*, she thought, whenever that would be.

Another week passed in a haze of tested nerves, aching feet and spent patience. The dream was so close, she could almost reach out and touch it. She'd managed to hold it together all this time, but now that the end was in sight, it was getting harder and harder to cope – like when you've been holding a wee in for ages without too much bother and the second you're in the vicinity of a toilet, you're suddenly walking like your legs are tied together and a little bit comes out.

As she trundled home at the end of another day, driven up the pole by customers asking for a bag after the transaction had gone through, with others miffed at simply being asked if they'd like a bag as though it were a dirty word, people arguing the toss to get the scabbiest discount and the initiation of Dawn's latest mind game (hiding rubbish around the store to see how vigilant staff really are) Sharon knew she was at the point of no return. 'Right, Gary! When, oh bloody when are we going to get these—' She ploughed through the sitting room door, trailing off as she found him sat on the sofa with a bottle of Moet & Chandon, a chipped wine glass, and the *twat of the year* mug she'd bought him for Christmas set out on the coffee table. He was grinning like a possum on crack and jangling something in the air.

'...*keys.*'

Hunky-dory

Chapter 5

'Hi Dawn, yeah. I'm just calling to say sorry for your loss.'

'My loss?'

'Yeah, *me*. As of now, I quit.'

'Well, sorry to burst your little bubble, Sharon, but I think you'll find that you're required to give two weeks' notice as per the terms and conditions of your contract.'

'And I think you'll find that I couldn't give a monkey's toss, Dawn. Ta-ra!'

Well, that's how she'd rehearsed it in her head, but it never went like that. It went something like this:

'Gaz, be a love and nip this into work for me, pretty please?'

'What is it?'

'My resignation.'

Although it would've been elation on the scale of a thousand orgasms all at once telling Dawn Turner to go fuck herself, Sharon refused to stoop to her level. A copied and pasted paragraph of undeserved professional niceties in Times New Roman was delicious enough all by itself; the wicked witch at last was dead!

When the landline started ringing early in the afternoon, Sharon wondered if it was Dawn calling for a whiney bitchfight. *Well, if it is, then she's going to have both barrels. If she doesn't like staff walking out, then she should bloody well …* 'Hello?'

'Oh, hello, love. Me and your dad were just wondering if you needed any help with the packing.' There followed an eruption of muddled, unintelligible whispers and hissing in the background from which Sharon was able to distinguish the words *foxtrot oscar, horseracing,* and *rotten sod.* 'Don't worry, Mum. Half of what we've got's fit for the bin so there really ain't much to pack. Let Dad watch his racing.'

'Ooh, yes. I suppose you'll be wanting to get everything new, won't you? How lovely,' she mused with a longing sigh. 'Such an exciting time for you both, all this good fortune. We're ever so pleased for you.'

'Aww, thanks Mum.'

'Well, let me know if you want any help cleaning down at the B&—' She trailed off and a guttural growl followed. 'Ohhh, pissing hell!'

'Mum? What is it? What's up?'

'Bloody Norma. At the window.' An almighty clamour erupted down the line. 'Watch the coffee table yer, daft apeth! Where yer going? I thought you said the racing was on?!' There followed a series of distant broad northern expletives and somewhere, a door slammed.

'D'ya know, I could kill him. Always sodding off and leaving me to deal with her!' She fumed. 'I'm only just speaking to him again after he knackered me Begonias.'

'How did he manage that?'

'Drowned the buggers. Look, I've gotta go, Norma de-potted me marigolds and posted them through the letterbox last time I took too long answering the door. I'll see you soon, love.' *Click.*

'Pack the handset when you're done on the blower, baby,' Gary called out from the hallway. 'I'm gonna start loading up the car. Izzy, sweetheart, pick those bleedin' fidget spinners up off the carpet, I'm trippin' over the buggers!'

Sharon placed the receiver down with a shiver of excitement. She had waited so long, and now, it was happening. It was really happening!

Clutching the now-clammy keys tightly in her fist, Sharon erupted into fits of elated squeals as they drew up outside the B&B. There it stood: dark and dishevelled, but full of the promise of sun-baked summers and cosy winters with all the trappings of beachside life. It wasn't just the place they would call home from now on, it was a childhood dream brought to life and tangible proof that – as nineties pop sensation, Gabrielle, would doubtless agree – dreams can come true.

She slid the key into the lock and gave it a turn. 'Woo-hoo! This is it guys, the first day of the rest of our lives!' The brand-spanking-new life she'd been dreaming of was waiting behind the door and all she had to do was walk through it.

Izzy sprinted straight upstairs to check out the bedrooms.

'Better get the windows open. Get some air into the place,' Sharon mused, bending down to pick up the crop of junk mail which was strewn across the doormat. As she blithely sifted through it, a large, white envelope caught her eye. Her fixed grin disintegrated as she observed the addressee's name. *'What?!'*

'What is it?' Gary's voice emanated from the lounge.

Sharon wandered in through the door and thrust the envelope toward him. 'This! It's that name again: *P. Goddard.'*

His eyes dipped uninterestedly toward the address label on the envelope. 'Oh, so it is.'

Sharon frowned. 'Don't you think it's a bit … spooky?'

'Spooky? Behave!' He mocked. 'There's bound ter be more than one *P. Goddard* in town.' He tucked the letter under his arm and nodded toward the corner. 'Good size room, this, innit? I reckon we could definitely stick a small bar in over there. Whaddya reckon?'

'Er … yeah, brilliant.'

'And we can stick a great big telly over there on that wall, couple of sofas here, some leather tub chairs and tables over th—'

'Er, the design side of things is my department, mister!' Sharon cut in, playfully wagging a finger. 'I've told you already, I do all the planning, you do all the doing.'

'Whatever you say, boss!' He chuckled, surveying the room with a gruntled grin. 'Tell yer what, this place is gunna be the dog's bollocks once we've put our mark on it. We are gunna be to the hospitality industry what Michael Bublé is to Christmas.'

'You think so?'

'I bloody know so!' He pulled her in for a smooch which wound up a peck when Izzy's voice came bouncing down the stairs. 'Muuuum, which bedroom's mine?'

They unstuck themselves. 'Ooh … hang on, I'll come up and we'll have a look.'

Gary pulled her back by her waistband. 'Here, give us the keys, baby. I'm just gunna have a quick recce out the back.'

She handed them over and joined Izzy on the stairs. 'This place is so cool, Mum! Do you know it has three whole staircases? Does that mean we're rich?'

Sharon laughed. 'Not quite.'

They surveyed the bedrooms on the top floor, wandering into one that looked out over the rear yard. 'Ooh. This is nice and bright. How about this one?'

Izzy wrinkled her nose up. 'No, I wanna wake up and see the sea!'

Sharon smiled lovingly at her little girl version. 'Whew, it's stuffy in here!' Wafting the air in front of her, she padded over to open the window and peered out across the back yard; already envisioning an artificial lawn, decking, rattan furniture and a pergola trussed in fairy lights where guests could sit and sip Shiraz under the stars.

'So, can I, Mum?'

'Shush.' Sharon put her ear toward the open window. She could hear a man talking, somewhere. He sounded executive, well-read, and serious all at the same time. She listened on, unable to make out what he was saying, but intrigued, nonetheless. Who was this mysterious new neighbour of theirs?

'Mum. Can I?'

'Izzy, shush a second.' Still straining to listen, Sharon did a double-take, blinking and blinking again as the source of the voice ambled down to the bottom of the yard, phone-to-ear … *it was Gary!*

A fortnight passed in a relentless cacophony of drilling and hammering, but finally, the B&B had metamorphosed from dreary dated digs to coastal crème de la crème. With its fancy, flocked wallpaper, crystal chandeliers, varnished wooden flooring, four poster beds, freestanding baths and shabby-chic furniture, the Driftwood would offer guests a touch of seaside luxury for a reasonable price.

Naturally, Pat the Donut Lady, who had turned up uninvited most days to see how the renovations were coming along, was the first over for a gander. 'Cor, you must've spent an absolute fortune on the place!' She gasped, her beady eyes dancing as Sharon gave her a guided tour of the downstairs.

'We've spent a few quid, but not as much as you'd think. I got a lot of the furniture pieces from classified ads and car boot sales. Jazzed 'em up myself. You'd be amazed what you can do with a bit of sandpaper and some spray paint.'

The disappointed look on Pat's face hinted that she'd been after more of a ballpark figure to relay back to the whole of Marine Parade. 'But it must've cost at least … hmmm, fifty grand?'

Sharon laughed. 'No, not that much. Anyway, come through, I'll show you the dining room.'

'*Thirty* grand, then?' Pat guessed, following hot on her tail.

'So, this is the dining room,' Sharon announced, loudly over the top of her. 'Gaz and I aren't the best at cooking but we wanted to offer a decent menu, so we've hired a chef.'

'*Twenty-five* grand?'

Jesus, does this nosy bag ever quit? Sharon's eyes darted looked toward the front window. 'Ooh! Looks like you've got a queue at the donut stall, Pat. You'd best be getting back.'

'Oh. Oh.' Pat mumbled, disappointedly as Sharon ushered her out in a maelstrom of clicking heels and jangling bangles. 'Never! It's never twenty grand?!' She tried one last time as Sharon closed the front door on her.

'Where are you off to?' She asked, as, just then, Gary ambled down the stairs in a potent cloud of Hugo Boss.

'I'm going to see me accountant, baby. Then I've got an appointment with the web designer, then I'm meeting Paul down the pub, so don't expect me back till late this evening.' He matched her disapproving look with one of his own. 'Look, baby. I've told yer! I ain't keepin' secrets from yer!'

'Well, you can't really blame me for thinking that, can you, Gary? You're always dashing off here and there. Then I overhear you on the phone, talking like some dude from "Bridgerton".'

'Ugh, how many more bloody times? I always put on a posh voice when I'm on the blower ter the bank. Everybody does. It ain't a crime.'

'Well … well, I just wish you'd include me more in things.'

'But I've only been looking out for you,

sweedheart! Taking care of all the boring bits so's you can get stuck into the redecorating. I know how much you enjoy all that stuff.'

Sharon's expression softened a little. She'd been crying out for Gary to take some initiative for as long as she could remember. She couldn't very well complain now that he had. 'When will you be back? I thought we could spend some quality time together before we open.'

'I dunno, baby. I won't say a time 'cos then I can't be late, can I?' He leaned forward and grabbed her by the waist. 'Listen, we've got all the time in the world for quality time. All the time in the world, baby. We're gonna make a success of this place and before yer know it, we'll be lying on a beach together somewhere in the Caribbean ... yeah? Hmm?' He pulled her close to his chest. 'Now, why don't yer get Trace over for some company? Open a bottle of wine. Make a night of it.'

She smiled, relentingly. 'Hm. I might just do that.'

'Well, I'll be dipped in shit! This place ain't half posh!' – it wasn't anymore!

'You like it?'

'Not half! I can't believe what you've done with the place! We could be in fackin' Mayfair!'

Sharon gave a modest chuckle. 'Come through to the lounge bar, I'll get us some drinks.'

Trace plonked her handbag onto the polished counter and settled into one of the plush chrome-based velvet knocker-back bar stools. 'And where's Gary tonight? Out on the piss, as per?'

Sharon gave an enervated sigh as she poured out two glasses of prosecco. 'He's been gone all day. Business appointments. Then he was meeting Paul down the pub.'

Trace raised a recently tattooed brow which resembled that of a Disney villain. 'Well, he ain't gunna be able to do much of that from now on, surely?'

Sharon slid a glass of fizz and a dubious look across the bar counter. 'Knowing Gary, he'll give it a bloody good try!' As she bent to place the Prosecco bottle in the fridge, something caught her eye. A wallet. A bulging brown leather wallet which she didn't recognise, tucked away among the rows of glasses. She picked it up and flipped it open, rifling through the conglomeration of cards ensconced inside. Sliding out a credit card, her face contorted in confusion as she observed a name she didn't recognise printed at the bottom: *Eric James.* 'What?'

Trace threw her a quizzical look. 'What's up?'

Sharon shook her head, dazedly, and flourished the wallet toward her. 'I've just found this hidden away between the glasses.'

Trace examined it, closely. 'Well, whose is it?'

'That's the thing, I haven't a clue. We don't know anyone by the name of Eric James.'

'Well, whoever he is, I could do with getting his number! He's obviously minted,' Trace marvelled, her glitter-tipped talons rifling through the bumper crop of notes tucked away inside.

Sharon stared at her glass, racking her brains for a plausible explanation.

'Might it be one of the workmen you've had in?' Trace offered.

'I dunno. Suppose so. I'll ping Gary a text. See if he knows.'

Trace nodded. 'Well, in other news, I've got meself a date this Saturday night.'

Sharon's face lit up as she tapped away on her phone. 'Ooooooh, really? Who is he?'

'He delivered me pizza from the Istanbul the other night. He asked if I was gunna eat it all by meself and I said *you bet yer bloody boots I am!* We got chatting. He told me he was single, and it all went from there, really.'

'Awesome! What's his name?'

'Balian.'

Sharon wrinkled her nose. '*Balian?* That's different.'

'Well, yeah, he's Turkish. But everyone calls him Barry.' As she said it, Sharon's mouth fell open and she almost dropped her phone. 'Oh, my God!'

'What is it? What's the matter with yer?'

'That Madame Whatsit said you were going to get with a Barry, remember?'

Trace clasped her hand to her mouth. 'Bloody hell! She did, didn't she? God. I'd better get me clout waxed and ready for action.'

A stunned silence ensued.

'Hm. Don't get too excited, though. I haven't forgotten the load of rot she told me in my reading,' Sharon reminded her.

'Alright, Christ. Don't spoil it!' Trace muttered, knocking back the rest of her glass. 'I haven't had a feel-up since Colin. I'm gagging for it.'

'Well, you never know, she might've been right about Barry,' Sharon offered, feeling pleased that she hadn't paid for her own reading just as a text came back from Gary...

Yeah, Eric and his boys did the flooring. I gave him a bell this morning and he's gunna come pick it up so just leave it where it is. I'll sort it. See you tonight x

'Ah! It's the floor fitters' wallet. Mystery solved!' Sharon declared, sounding relieved.

Trace rapped her nails thoughtfully on the counter. 'Well, if it doesn't work out with Barry, then perhaps your Gaz can set me up with this Eric fella?'

Finally, opening day arrived, and the first couple of weeks of working for themselves as B&B hosts would prove to be the calm before the storm for the Blewitts. After which, the floodgates seemed to open overnight and bookings went through the roof – partly thanks to a local travel vlogger, *Walk With Me Tim*, who, unbeknownst to the Blewitts, had taken an overnight stay with his wife and uploaded a glowing vlog to his YouTube.

Driftwood's Tripadvisor listing was soon awash with applauding reviews for the *affordable taste of luxury* and *friendly, personal experience* it offered guests.

The Great Yarmouth Mercury ran a piece branding it a *hidden pearl* and the phone was ringing non-stop with hopefuls looking for last-minute cancellations. Sharon had to take down the vacancies sign, which didn't go back up until winter because the Driftwood was always full. Business was booming!

The Blewitts were making money hand over fist and the bank and finance companies were falling over themselves to lend to them … well, to Sharon – Gary's credit score was through the floor.

Before too long, their success showed. Gone was their clapped-out Ford Focus with the gaffer-taped wing mirror and, in its place, a brand new, shiny SUV complete with parking camera and all the mod cons. Then there was the Shark cordless vacuum, the effing great telly, the latest generation Echo dot, the Ring doorbell, the winter trip to Centre Parcs, the matching PJs at Christmas – *yes*, they were that family, they just hadn't known it yet.

Sharon started getting her hair done properly at the hairdressers instead of colouring it with *2 for £7* box dyes and attempting to trim it with the massive kitchen scissors. She dressed in power suits and no longer had to worry about what the hospital would think if she were ever to be run over and blue-lighted in, because now, her knickers were hole-less and had full elastic. With her underwear drawer overflowing with brightly coloured matching sets, she could get run over all she liked, now!

Gary also updated his wardrobe and, for some reason, started dressing like a Peaky Blinder.

The Blewitts were going up in the world, and everybody could see it; nobody more so than The Godmothers who now went out of their way to talk to Sharon. Suddenly, an endless batch of party invitations seemed to appear like magic in Izzy's Harry Potter backpack and the days that Sharon would slip in unnoticed to a deserted corner of the playground were long gone. Now, her status as a seafront trader had earned her honeyed *hiyaaaaaahs* and breathless invites to their coffee mornings – not that she ever took them up on it, of course. The Godmothers, after all, were faker than Benidorm beachfront Louis Vuitton and, in all honesty, Sharon would sooner have put a campfire out with her face than have anything to do with them.

Gradually, Gary stopped going away at the weekends and seldom went to the pub, instead, preferring to host his friends in the lounge bar or garden. It was just like old times, but better. The old sayings were wrong: money *is* everything! Life is much more more fun and so much easier when you have it. It seemed to add a touch of sparkle to everything; every little aspect of their lives. The couple couldn't pass each other in the hallway without Gary giving his wife's bottom a cheeky squeeze. The sex doubled to twice a week. They were holding hands again, hugging, flirting, even. The man Sharon had fallen in love with was back... All was well in her happy place.

Tempest

Chapter 6

June 2021, Great Yarmouth Police Station.

As she approached the entrance door, Sharon cleared her throat for the seventeenth time since getting out of the car. Whatever Gary had done or *not* done, she prayed that it would be an easy fix – though the feeling deep within the pit of her stomach was telling her different. The door opened with a squeak, and she clawed at her windswept hair as she approached the front desk. *This is crazy! What am I doing here?*

A bearded chap with glasses looked up from behind the glass on her approach. 'Can I help, madam?'

'Um … yeah. My husband was brought in earlier and I've been asked to come in to help with your enquiries?' She peered around, tensely, and lowered her voice to even smaller proportions. 'It's

Sharon Blewitt.'

The ensuing look on his face suggested that the name was already fabled within the station. 'Ah, yes!' He clicked his fingers and rose from his chair. 'I'll let the detectives know you're here.'

A stab of alarm hit as the word repeated in her mind: *Detectives?* Shit. This was serious stuff. It had to be with detectives involved.

Oh, God. Please don't let him have done anything stupid! As Sharon fixed her eyes upon – but did not read – the posters on the wall, her thoughts raced, pulse thumped, throat tightened. It was a feeling which had no place in her new, comfy, padded world. *It's all a big mistake. Someone's messed up, somewhere. Just please, don't let it be Gary!*

A serious voice and a sequence of footsteps made her jump. 'Hello Mrs Blewitt, I'm Detective Inspector Crawley and this is Detective Inspector Hart. Thank you for coming in,' said the older chap of the two. He pulled his fingers through his ginger beard and motioned toward a set of double doors. 'If you'd like to come through to the interview room.'

No. She wouldn't. She wouldn't bloody well like to at all! But she followed them on tenterhooks. 'Um … do you know where my husband is? Will he be kept in much longer? It's just that we've got a daughter and the business to…'

'We'll explain everything inside, Mrs Blewitt.'

'Call me Sharon.' *Please! For the love of God, call*

me fucking Sharon!

She followed their lead through to the interview room, cautiously conscious that every second away from the B&B was another weight/bowel/sex-life complaint for Trace to be sharing with the guests. It was good of her to help out in a crisis, but, knowing Trace, it would be less *service with a smile*, more *service with no filter*.

'Take a seat.'

Sharon lowered herself hesitantly and perched on the edge of the chair, hands clasped at the knees. *Please let this be quick!*

In contrast, both detectives eased themselves into their chairs in a way that suggested they were there for the long haul.

'Okay, before we begin Sharon, I do just need to let you know that the interview is being recorded. You have the right to legal representation if you wish. You can end the interview at any time, and you don't have to say anything, but anything you do say may be given in evidence.' D.I Crawley's voice was professional, but he seemed to have a Buddha-like calm about him. 'Would you like legal representation, Sharon?'

She curled her lip. 'Well, given that I haven't broken the law in any way and I've no idea why I'm here, I can't see why I'd need it.'

'Right, then. We'll begin.'

She tapped a foot, nervously, on the low-profile carpet.

'Could you tell me when you and your husband

acquired the Driftwood Bed and Breakfast?'

'We got the keys in May. Last year.'

'Okay. And could you tell me how you acquired the business, i.e. how you purchased it?'

'Yes, my husband put half the asking price down in cash as a deposit and took out a commercial mortgage on the other half.' She noticed the fleeting elevation of D.I Crawley's bushy, ginger brows.

D.I Hart cleared his throat. 'Sharon, would it be fair to say that prior to the purchase of your business, yourself and your husband were struggling financially?' His voice had a sharp edge to it, and he was looking at her as though he was trying to catch her out in some way.

'Yes, that's right, we were.'

He glanced briefly at the notes on the table in front of him. 'So, would you mind telling me how it was that you came up with one hundred and eighty thousand pounds cash to pay down as the deposit?' His arms were folded, and his tone came across as accusatory. Either he was relatively new to the job and trying too hard, or, like a lot of people in positions of power, he was a bellend. Sharon wasn't sure which. By now, the arse of her trousers was stuck to the plastic seat of her chair, and she was sweating in places she hadn't known could sweat. *How the bloody hell would I cope if I'd actually broken the law?* She wondered. She cleared her throat. 'Gary inherited some money in his uncle's will, and he used that.'

D.I Hart smirked. 'Could you tell us about the will you're referring to?'

'It was his Uncle Ted's estate, and he was only one of three people named in the will.' She watched as he took a pen from his shirt pocket and added to the notes on the table in unreadable scrawl.

'Do you know much he was left?

'Half a million, he reckoned.'

He smirked again. 'And did you ever see any evidence of this er … will?'

'No. He said his aunt was the executor and he'd met her at the solicitors to sign all the paperwork. He'd wanted to keep it from me until the last minute so that it was all a big surprise.'

'And presumably nothing ever came through the post?'

'No. Nothing.'

'And did you not think that strange?' D.I Hart was really beginning to piss her off and the tone of her reply let him know this. 'Look … he had an answer for everything, okay? I didn't question it. Especially when he showed me what was left of the cash in the bank after he'd bought the B&B. The money sort of spoke for itself. You don't just pluck money like that out of thin air, do you?'

A short silence ensued.

'Did you have access to the bank account, Sharon?' D.I Crawley interjected, softly.

'No. He'd opened a new account of his own which the cheque was paid into. I didn't know about this account till he told me later down the line.'

'Did he explain why he'd gone to the lengths of opening a separate account?'

Sharon dragged her mind back. 'Well, he'd said it was all planned to be a big surprise ... for *me*. I'd always spoken about us having our own business and he said that as soon as he'd found out about the inheritance, he knew straight away that he was going to buy a B&B with the money. And, given that it was a surprise, he'd had to keep the funds hidden.' She bit her lip. Why were they looking at her like that? 'Look. I was going through a cancer scare at the time. My mind had been fully on that,' she added.

D.I Crawley gave an empathic nod. 'And what about the sale agreement for the B&B. Did he show you any of the paperwork?'

Sharon shook her head. 'No. He'd taken care of all that by himself before I'd even known about it. You know, with it being a surprise and that.' How many more times did she have to say it?

He gave an acknowledging grunt. 'Okay. I'd like you to think back now, Sharon. Think hard. Do you recall, at any point around that time, any strange behaviour on your husband's part?'

What, Gary Blewitt who kept his socks on during lovemaking? He didn't just *act* strange, he was a strange person! Just ... Gary, really. She stared down at her feet as she cast her mind back to spring of the previous year. 'Well, the day he told me about the inheritance and the B&B, I was just about to leave him. I'd had a case packed ready by the door. Things hadn't been good between us for a long time.'

'How so?'

A showreel of events from what now felt like another life replayed in her mind. 'He was distant. We barely spoke. He wouldn't touch me. He was always out down the pub and away at the weekends.'

'And where did he go at the weekends?'

'All over the place. He was playing in pool tournaments.'

D.I Hart's posture changed. He looked more sympathetic … and slightly disappointed.

'I told him I was leaving and that's when he told me everything,' she added.

D.I Hart sat forward in his chair. 'Did you stay with him for the money, Sharon?'

Her face ruckled. '*No!* No, it wasn't about the money. It was the change in circumstance. He reckoned we'd only drifted apart because of our circumstances and that the money would give us a fresh start, make it all better. He was literally on his knees begging me to try again. I'm a mother! I agreed to give it one last shot for our daughter's sake.'

D.I Hart slumped back into his chair and D.I Crawley's sudden awkward clearing of his throat was enough hint to there being a bombshell imminent.

'I'm sorry to have to inform you Sharon, but the information we have on your husband suggests he has committed major fraud.'

'Sorry?!'

He lowered his voice to its softest tone yet. 'He wasn't playing in pool tournaments when he was away at the weekends. He was involved romantically with women up and down the country ... women he was defrauding.'

BAM! He might as well have punched her straight in the stomach.

'All of them wealthy, all of them widowed.' D.I. Hart added.

The room started to spin. She felt sick. *Gary? Romantically involved? Widows?!* She recoiled in shock, half expecting to hear the Eastenders duff duffs because this was the stuff of a bloody soap plot!

'Sharon, did you ever suspect that your husband might not have been telling you the truth about his inheritance?'

She felt the blood drain from her face, whilst the bile rose in her throat.

'Are you okay? Do you want to stop for a minute?'

She shook her head.

'For the purpose of the recording, Mrs Blewitt is shaking her head.'

Ms. Taylor, now!

D.I Hart sank back into his chair again and twirled his pen around his fingers. 'Sharon, we have reason to believe that your husband obtained the funds he passed off as inheritance through romance fraud.'

'W-what?'

'He stole the money from his victims.'

Her mouth seemed to open and close repeatedly in the moments that followed. 'But Gary's not … how could he pull any of this off? He left school with one GCSE. He thinks Welsh rarebit is cheese on toast, for God's sake!'

A slight snigger erupted from D.I Hart. 'It *is*.'

'Pardon?'

'Well, it is basically cheese on toast.'

Her brow creased in surprise. 'Is it? I thought it was rabbit from Wales.'

They were both looking at her sympathetically now.

'Sharon, your husband is a master manipulator. He met these women on dating websites and managed to convince them that he was an MI5 agent from London called Eric James,' D.I Crawley revealed.

Boom! *The wallet. The credit cards. The name.* Suddenly, the jigsaw pieces were slotting together.

'This is how he was able to get away with appearing, and disappearing. They put it down to his job, and obviously, his job title would have gone some way to making these ladies feel that they could trust him.'

'And 'this is how he managed to obtain their financial details. He would tell them that everything they did together had to be booked and paid for in their names rather than his, given the nature of his job. Of course, they willingly handed over debit and credit card information to him which he then exploited. Squirreling away funds here and there from each of them, giving out the impression he was wealthy himself.'

OMG, the Bridgerton voice!

'He was wining and dining them with their own money.'

Sharon stared at D.I Hart's stripey socks as she tried to take all this in; her brain more fried than a fish supper from PJ's.

The trips away. His stagnant libido. His expert knowledge in dining etiquette. His excellence in king prawn dismemberment. The alarm bells had been ringing away in the background, but she'd had her fingers stuck in her ears the whole time. Ignored the little voice within ... the one that's never wrong. Gary had played her like a slot machine at The Silver Slipper!

How could I have been so bloody stupid?! 'So ... s-so, what happens now?'

'Well, he's denying it all, of course. But we've more than enough evidence to charge him. Particularly now we've got your side. He'll be remanded in custody until the trial date.'

Sharon drew in a sharp breath. 'Remanded in custody?'

D.I Crawley gave a resounding nod. 'Given the seriousness of his crimes, yes. We aren't just looking at romance fraud, here. We're looking at credit card fraud, identity theft, mortgage fraud; the list goes on.'

'Wait … *mortgage* fraud?'

He nodded. 'Mr Blewitt obtained a commercial mortgage in one of his victim's names. I'm afraid this means that you don't own the B&B.'

Sharon's heart seemed to freeze in her chest as the words assimilated: the Blewitt's little pot of gold had been someone else's. 'S-so, who does … own it?'

His gaze flicked to his notes and back. 'A Mrs Pamela Goddard.'

A thousand lightbulbs seemed to flash on inside her head all at once. *P. Goddard!*

'But obviously, the mortgage isn't valid. So, the mortgage lender is the legal owner, and it will seek to repossess the property,' he continued.

The words hit like a ton of bricks. They were going to lose the business. Their home. *Everything.*

'B-but … we have a child. We've sold our house. What am I going to do?'

D.I Crawley lowered his head and said nothing.

'One thing you do have is your freedom, Sharon,' D.I Hart offered. 'Your husband's going to do a good stretch in prison. His life's as good as finished for the foreseeable.' And in that moment, Sharon knew that hers would be, too.

'Sorry, love. We thought you were Norma,' a flustered-looking Sue greeted Sharon at the front door having spent the last ten minutes hiding behind the armchair. 'You can come out, it's only our Sharon,' she bellowed, prompting the gradual surfacing of Izzy's head from behind the TV unit. 'What's going on, then? What did the police want with you?'

Sharon braced herself to speak, pausing in surprise momentarily as Jim crawled out on his knees from behind the sofa. He shook his head, indignantly. 'Don't mind me. Carry on.'

She turned toward Izzy who was blinking back at her in anticipation. How, exactly, do you tell an eleven-year-old child that her father has been living a double life? That her toy collection to rival Kerrison's is as good as nicked and they've all been living a dirty, rotten lie? Eventually, it all came tumbling out in a torrent of heavy sobs.

For a good minute, nobody said a word and they all sat in stunned silence. Eventually, Jim broke it. 'Well, of all the lying … cheating … thieving ….' He paused, teeth clenched, face reddening as he fished for a fitting word, '….COCKWOMBLES!'

'JIM! Not in front of our Izzy,' Sue scolded, reaching for her fags from the arm of the sofa.

'I could say a lot bloody worse!'

'Well, *don't*!'

He shook his head and begrudgingly buttoned his lip – for now.

'Is Dad in jail?' Izzy asked.

'Yes, love. I'm afraid he is,' Sue replied, reaching forward, and placing a soothing hand on her shoulder.

'Does that mean we can't go to Pleasurewood Hills at the weekend?'

'Oh, I shouldn't think so, love.'

'Awww, fuck's sake!'

'IZZY!' All three of them chorused at once.

'So, what happens now, love?' Sue asked, looking desperately at Sharon who gave a defeated shrug.

'It's over, Mum. We're going to lose everything.'

'But, what about the business? It's doing so well! Can you not ask the mortgage company if they'd let you carry it on and take over the repayments yourself?'

'They'll not go for that,' Jim vetoed with a firm headshake.

'Why?'

'Give over, woman! You think the mortgage lender gives two hoots about our Sharon? That arsewipe has gone and committed mortgage fraud. All they'll care about is getting their cash back in full as quickly as they can. Draw a line in the sand.'

'Well, it's worth an ask, Jim, surely?'

'Don't be bloody daft! There's nowt in the place that's rightfully theirs. Pretty soon, it'll be all over't local bloody press. Oh, come and 'ave a relaxing brek at the Driftwood in a stolen feckin' bed fer yers' 'olidays,' he mocked. 'The whole town's gonna get to know about it. She's better walking away from it all.'

Sue peered down at her fluffy pink slippers, defeatedly. 'Dearie me. It's all one great big bloody mess, isn't it?'

High and Dry

Chapter 7

The marker pen squeaked upon the square of glossy scrap card as Sharon finished up writing the makeshift notice in block caps: *CLOSED FOR BUSINESS.* She fixed it to the dining room window with a hunk of Blu Tack and a sigh , and stared out onto the dusky seafront. It was hard to think that in the space of a year, she'd had it all and lost it – and even harder *still* to know that it had never been hers to begin with. She'd been living on borrowed time, and now, she'd timed out.

Just as she'd concluded that things could not get any worse, Stella drew up outside in her Noddy car with a jerk and a squeaking of brakes.

Huffing in disbelief, Sharon watched as she clambered out and strode toward the front door of the B&B; skirt swishing, limp missing in action.

'This is all your fault,' she accused, before the door had even fully opened. Her words were loaded with malice.

'Pardon?'

She wagged a bony finger in Sharon's face. 'You

were always pushing him. You couldn't just be satisfied with the life you had, could you? Oh, no! You were always there in his ear. Nagging him! Wanting more! You pushed him to the limit. *You* made him do this!'

Sharon's eyes widened in dismay. 'Don't you blame me for your son's actions. I'm as much a victim in this as anyone else!'

'He only did it for you!'

'You, what?! Doinking a load of rich widows for *me*?! Give your bloody head a wobble, Stella! Everything Gary did was for his own ends, and if you're looking for someone to blame, I suggest you look a bit closer to home.'

Her scowl doubled in depth. 'And what is *that* supposed to mean?!'

'Well, he's learned from the master, hasn't he?'

Stella's nostrils flared like a dragon's, and her thin, pruney lips curled in contempt as she drew back her hand and slapped Sharon hard around the face. 'How dare you?!'

Clutching her stinging cheek, Sharon slapped her straight back.

A scuffling of heels resounded as Stella stumbled off the step from the force, before straightening up and landing her nemesis with another dry slap which, again, was duly returned in a scene that briefly reminded Sharon of the beginning of the music video to New Order's "True Faith."

The pair froze in shock, faces on fire as they

glowered at one another. Sharon lost the stare-off as her eyes instinctively flicked toward the little pink donut hut with a not-so-little head gawking out of its serving hatch, eyes out on stalks. Time seemed to stand still, and Sharon could almost hear the theme from *The Good, The Bad and The Ugly* as she pointed confrontationally toward it. 'Do you want some, an' all?!'

Pat's frosted-pink lips fell agape as the front door to the B&B slammed shut with a reverberating bang.

Sharon wedged the suitcase into the last of the available space and closed the car boot aggressively, wishing briefly that her mother-in-law's head had been beneath it. With a wistful sigh, she took one last glance at the B&B: her passion, her livelihood, her baby. In the relatively short time in which the Blewitts had run it, she'd invested her heart and soul into the place. *She* was the one who'd gotten their top Tripadvisor rating. It was the extras. The thoughtful little touches. None of that had been Gary's doing. No. His little touches had been for his wealthy widows. And now, here she was, bags packed and leaving – not on a jet plane, but in a white Nissan Qashqai she would never be able to keep up the repayments on – and she felt robbed, as though she'd spent an age building this massive, palatial sandcastle only for some sod to come along and jump on it.

As she gazed, longingly, at the postcard-perfect B&B standing before a dusky backdrop of pink-lavender ombre, it really was like watching the sun set on her dreams.

Echoes of Gary's fanfaronade lapped at the shore of her mind: *we are gunna be to leisure and tourism what Michael Bublé is to Christmas!* Hmph! More like what Ronnie Biggs was to Royal Mail.

Clambering into the front seat, she was pleased to observe that the pink donut hut was also closed for business. Though the passers-by having a bloody good gawk more than made up for nosy Pat's absence.

'Izzy, will you get in the bloody car?!'

As they pulled away sharper than planned with Bananarama's "Cruel Summer" blaring out on Harbour Radio, Sharon had a feeling that this would be the cruellest yet.

She changed gear with brute force and bashed the button for the next station.

'Are we going to see Dad again?' Izzy called out from the back seat.

Sharon hesitated. 'I'm ... not sure.'

'Even though he's a cheating cockwomble?'

Thanks for that, Dad. Bloody nice one!

They cruised along in silence, until, in a cruel twist of fate, the first bars of Savage Garden's "Truly Madly Deeply" rang out. Of all the bloody songs to come on the radio in the short five-minute drive from the seafront to her folks' place! As if fate hadn't bloodied her nose enough today already.

Izzy groaned exasperatedly from the back seat as her mother began to howl, swathes of pent-up tears finally surfacing. 'This was mine and your dad's song,' she wailed, with minimal thought to how she must look to the oncoming traffic.

As they took a left down St Nicholas Road and passed the corner shop, she was confronted by a bold, black headline displayed upon the news stand: *local bed & breakfast host charged with fraud.* Boom! The cat was out of the bag.

'Come, on in. I'm doing Shephard's Pie for tea,' Sue fussed, ushering Sharon and Izzy inside as they arrived on the doorstep in a tangle of holdalls and suitcases. Sharon cringed inwardly as blinds jostled and curtains twitched in the neighbouring houses. 'It's made headline news, Mum.'

'I know, love. Your dad's been out and bought The Mercury.'

Sharon's mouth fell open. 'Wow. Thanks a bunch!'

'Ooh, give over. He always buys it. It's just unfortunate that your life's plastered over the front page this edition. Anyway, it doesn't mention you. It only mentions him and the business.'

'That'll not stop tongues wagging around 'ere,' Jim announced gruffly over the top of the newspaper. 'She'll be guilty by association.'

'D'ya know, I feel so much bloody better for coming here!' Sharon fizzed, dropping onto the sofa in a peeved heap.

'Well … it is what it is,' Jim muttered, matter-of-factly, as he flicked through the pages.

'Don't worry, it'll all be fish and chip wrapping tomorrow, love.' Sue's attempt at motherly reassurance resonated from the kitchen.

Jim pulled a mocking face. He may have loved the beach, but he wasn't one for burying his head in the sand.

Suddenly, Sharon's handbag started to vibrate. Her face crumpled in confusion as she fished her phone from it. 'That's a Norwich number. Who could it be?'

'Here's an idea, bloody answer it and find out,' Jim suggested, coolly.

'But I don't know the number. It might be the press.'

'Get it answered!'

'Hello?'

'Shaz. Baby! It's me.' Her face fell straight as she heard his voice. 'What do you want?'

'I need you, sweedheart. I want you to come and see me. You and Izzy. They've moved me. I'm doing porridge in Norwich.'

'No, Gary.'

Jim's head shot up, meerkat-like from behind his newspaper. 'Is that him? Is that feckin' him?'

Sharon gave an inflamed, confirmatory nod.

'Look, baby. I don't know what they've told you, but it ain't what you think,' Gary pleaded. 'They're trying to fix me up for all sorts. At least give me the chance to tell my side.'

She snorted in dismay. 'Save it, Gary. I'm not interested in hearing any more of your bullshit lies. It's over.'

An irked sigh resonated down the line. 'At least bring Izzy to see me. You can't stop me seeing our daughter.'

'I haven't. You've managed to do that all by yourself!'

Jim started thrashing around in his chair like an angry croc. 'Give me that bloody phone. I've a thing or two t'say to him!'

Sharon switched the phone to her other ear with a huff. 'Look, if Izzy wants to see you, I'll bring her. But I wouldn't hold your breath,' she told him, hanging up.

'He's got some feckin' nerve! What was that all about?' Jim looked furious.

'He wants to see me and Izzy.'

'Well, he can get stoofed!'

'Pipe down, Jim. It'll be up to our Izzy if she wants to see her dad or not,' Sue argued, wafting through from the kitchen. 'Anyway, the shed wants clearing out.'

His head turned sharply toward her. 'But "TippingPoint"'s on!'

'You're not even watching it!'

'I am!'

'No, you're bloody not!'

Sharon closed her eyes in pre-emptive dread. A fraught five-second silence ensued.

'If that shed's not cleared by supper, you'll be sleepin' in the bugger tonight!'

'Agh, get stoofed, woman!' Jim hissed, rising from the armchair in a tussle of crumpling newspaper. He slapped the Mercury down onto the coffee table and strode off.

'If you walk out that door—'

Slam!

'Right! I've 'ad it with him. That's his lot. His goose is cooked!' Sue scowled, stomping back to the kitchen. They both knew Jim's goose had been burning its arse off for nigh on forty years, just as they also knew that they'd be sat with their feet up watching Corrie that evening as if nothing had happened. Their rows were like petrol price hikes: came out of nowhere for no good reason and, though decades had passed since Sharon had lived at home, nothing had changed. It was just like old times. Had Madame Catharina told her there would be a marriage break-up in the family, Sharon would've bet everything she had on it being her folks. But though they fought like cat and dog, remarkably, they kept buggering on. It was peculiar. Theirs was no Jane Austen romance, that's for bloody sure. It'd been a love-hate relationship from day one.

Back in 1975, Sue had worked as a ticket girl at

the old Royalty cinema. Jim, a Yorkshire lad, was on a bank holiday beano to Yarmouth with the lads. They'd all gone to see "Jaws." He'd swaggered past the ticket booth afterwards, saw her looking down in the dumps, and rather than resort to the usual *cheer up, might never happen*, or similar, he'd taken aim with his imaginary rifle, and in the words of Chief Brody, told her *smile, you son of a bitch!* At least with Jim, what you saw was what you got, which had not been the case with Gary.

After tea, with the shed still rammed to the rafters with crap, soaps on, feet up and brews all round, Sharon's phone began to flash like a lighthouse on the coffee table. A bolt of dread surged through her. People would be sitting down for the evening, catching up on the news. The whispering campaign had begun...

> *Hey Hun. Just seen the news. R U ok? xx*
>
> *Sharon, OMG! Call me! x*
>
> *What's happened babes? xxx*
>
> *Hope you're ok? x*

She hadn't heard a dickie bird from these people in months, but now they were popping up like surfers, all agog.

'A listening ear's a running mouth,' Jim cautioned. 'Don't spill the tea.' He was right. Nobody was interested to know that you were doing alright. They wanted to hear that you'd gone bankrupt. That you'd put on six stone. That your husband had left you for someone ten years younger with bigger funbags.

Sharon knew her life was about to play out like a circus show at the Hippodrome. In the days to come, the speculative looks across the aisles in Boots and whispers in the marketplace would only serve to confirm that the show was a sell-out. The whole town was there, armed with popcorn and watching eagerly in the wings.

Awoken by the usual anarchic clamour of the seagulls the next morning, Sharon could easily have been waking up at the Driftwood with the drama of the week all but a harrowing dream … until she rolled over and fell out of the bed she'd quite forgotten she was in; one of the two spot-patterned singles in her folks' spare room which barely afforded her a quarter of the rolling space that her former marital super king had. If adult-Sharon waking in teen-Sharon's bedroom with her daughter in the bed opposite wasn't weirdly nostalgic enough, then Jim's footsteps thundering up the stairs moments later – just as they did whenever The Prodigy was blaring too loudly from her nineties' ghetto blaster – only added to the feeling. She could almost have been that same girl with the spiral perm and permanent scowl as his bulky frame appeared in blue pinstripe pyjamas, hands-on-hips in the doorway.

'What the bleedin' eck's goin' on, Sharon? I thought the feckin' ceilin' were comin' through!'

'Fell out of bed,' she muttered, half expecting to be grounded.

She peered toward Izzy who was staring down from the sanctuary of the bed opposite looking nonplussed and quickly put on her mum-face. 'Morning sweets, did you sleep okay?'

'Er, no!'

'Why?' She asked, fearful of the effect all of this might be having on her. 'Because you kept crying and sniffing. Then you started snoring. *Then*, you did a massive fart in your sleep!'

Sharon huffed in surprise. She'd assumed that sleeping with her mum would've been a comfort to the child, but apparently she was the only one around here in need of that.

'Would you rather I walked Izzy to school, love?' Sue asked from the kitchen table over a mouthful of toast. 'You know, just while it's all still fresh.'

Sharon shook her head as she set about fixing Izzy's Frosties. 'No, it's okay, Mum. They're going to see me sooner or later. No point prolonging the inevitable.'

'Hear! Hear!' Jim's voice resonated from the armchair in the sitting room. 'Life is like riding a bicycle. To keep yer balance, you've gotta keep moving.'

Sue stopped munching and went all googly eyed. 'Ooh, he's good, ain't he?'

'Einstein!' Sharon coughed.

There came a brief pause.

'People can't hurt you without your permission,' he added, safe in the knowledge that Sue had never heard of Mahatma Gandhi.

Sharon repeated the Gandhi-born mantra under her breath as she and Izzy manoeuvred head-down past the blockade of spandex at the school gates, wondering if they'd be stopped and given forged looks of concern and counterfeit condolences. But they didn't say a word. They didn't have to. The looks on their faces said enough.

She continued walking, even when somebody started whistling *The Ballad of Bonnie and Clyde*.

It was no surprise that The Godmothers were talking. Scandal was their fuel. They licked their lips at the slightest whiff of it, and here was a feast big enough to feed them for months.

What irked Sharon most about all of this was that none of it was *her* doing. She wasn't the perpetrator. The shame was purely Gary's, his price to pay. Yet somehow, they were going Dutch.

Scraping the Barrel

Chapter 8

'You sure you wanna do this?' Sharon asked cautiously through the interior mirror.

'Yeah,' Izzy shrugged from the back seat.

'You're definitely sure? Prisons aren't nice places, you know,' – a sentiment soon confirmed when, minutes later, she was accosted by a sniffer dog with a fondness for crotches. Sharon hadn't needed this, nor to be standing scarecrow-like while a prison guard patted her down to feel like a criminal. She'd felt like one every day since Gary's house of cards had come tumbling down.

As they were given the nod to enter the visiting room, she spotted him sat hunched at a table with his back to them. She'd spent many a lonesome night staring at the back of that nut enough to recognise it instantly.

His posture straightened as Izzy arrived first at the table. 'Iz! Oh, baby, come here!' He swept her into a bear hug and held her tightly to his chest.

As she pulled up a chair, Sharon could barely bring herself to look at him.

"Ello, Shaz.' She kept her eyes fixed firmly to the table. 'Thanks for coming baby. Knew yer wouldn't let me down.'

'I ain't here for you!' She hissed, head jerking in outrage.

'Look, I know you hate me right now, but just hear me out, yeah?'

'I'm not here to hear you out, Gary. I've been hearing you out for nigh on twenty-four years. I'm not interested in anything you've got to say.' She snatched her arm away as his hand snaked across the table.

'Just listen to me Shaz. Just listen, baby,' his tone was desperate. 'I'm being fitted up, here. I ain't done none of it.' He peered around and lowered his voice to a covert whisper. 'Ma's pushing for bail. I'm gonna be out of here soon, okay? Then, we're gonna get some passports knocked up and we're gonna get on a plane and we're gonna go and live somewhere hot, yeah? Just you, me, Izzy, and Ma.'

Sharon looked as though she'd been bitten by a shark. The Gary Blewitt she had known couldn't organise a prayer in a mosque, but this one could get hold of four fake passports? 'You're living in Cloud Cuckoo Land! The fact that you think you're gonna walk out of here on bail after everything you've done is insane enough, but thinking we can all just live together abroad like the pissing Waltons on the run ... with your arsehole bloody mother?! You're off your nut!' She told him in breathless disbelief.

He frowned back at her. 'Why are you being like this? I need yer support. I need me wife standing by me side. For better for worse, remember?' He said it with a sort of faux sincerity.

She stared across the table at him and felt nothing. After all, the man she'd loved had been fictional. This was just the actor she was looking at, and she didn't know him from Adam.

Her sarcastic laughter erupted louder than planned across the room, prompting a suspicious glare from the guard. 'Well, it's a shame you didn't think of that when you were off banging widows for their savings.'

He shook his head. 'I've told yer, Shaz. They're fitting me up. I'm innocent.'

She studied him through a stony gaze. 'Look at you. Still lying through your teeth after everything!'

'I ain't lying, Shaz,' he insisted, 'they've got the wrong bloke. It's a case of mistaken identity. It happens!'

'Yeah, it does. Like the night you went out with the wrong wallet you prat! I saw it with my own eyes, Gary. Or should I call you Eric? Which is it? Who are you? Do you even know? 'Cos I'm buggered if I do.'

He slumped back in his chair, defeatedly.

'There's no way out of this. You might as well give me the truth. It's the least you owe me.'

He let out his breath and scratched the back of his head. 'Alright, look ...' he glanced around cautiously and kept his voice low. 'When you said you was leaving, I panicked. I didn't wanna lose you and Izzy, so I had ter think of something on the spot ter make you stay and the story about the inheritance and buying the B&B was the only thing I could think of.'

She stared at him incredulously. 'So, there was no B&B all along?'

He shook his head. 'I had ter run out and buy the bugger, after.'

Well, that would explain a lot! 'And these ...' Sharon trailed off and glanced at Izzy, mindfully. 'These other women?'

'Started as a bit of fun at first. Just wanted ter see if I could still pull,' he laughed.

She shook her head in disbelief.

'So, I signed up to this dating website and got a message from this older bird,' he continued, 'turned out she was a widow, proper minted, and I was curious ter see where it went. I told you I was playing in pool tournaments, but I wasn't, obviously. Matter of fact, I'm crap at pool.' He chuckled. 'Anyway, I give her this cock and bull story about working for MI5 and she fell for it. Trusted me without question. Daft cow even gave me her online banking login. Let me pay fer stuff with her bank card. I started helping meself to the dough and she never noticed. None of 'em did. It was a piece of piss. These rich old mares got that much moolah, they don't even notice bits going out here and there. I was stashing some away for a rainy day and using the rest of it ter take them out. Hehe, took 'em ter fancy restaurants with their own dosh, imagine that? Anyway, it got addictive. I started getting involved with others and it all spiralled out of control. Guess I got greedy. Then you was gunna leave me and I had ter pull something big outta the bag. That's when it all went tits-up, really.'

Sharon sat, stunned. 'If you care so much about me and Izzy, why weren't we enough for you? Why did you have to do this?'

He shrugged. 'It was fun.' His tone held not a single note of remorse.

Wow. Who was this sociopath? Who was the man behind the mask, masquerading as *Gaz*? *Gaz the joker. Gaz the clumsy clown.* Sharon didn't know. All she knew was that he was heartless. Dead behind the eyes.

'It was only ever about the dough, Shaz. These birds meant nothing ter me. It was purely about the money, I swear it!'

She gave a throaty chuckle. 'You swear it, do you? Well, that means sod all! You, Gary Blewitt, are a pathological liar. And you've no hope in hell of getting bail, so I hope you like prison food because it's gonna be a long time before you see another king prawn!' She stood up, her chair sliding out behind her with an unpleasant scraping sound. 'Come on, Izzy. Let's go.'

'Bye, Dad,' she mumbled, following suit.

'No, wait!' He begged. 'If you leave me now, you'll

take away the biggest part of me.'

Sharon threw him a look of disgust. 'You don't care about us. We should never have come. It was just another of your ploys to … and can we *stop* with the bloody song lyrics?! It didn't work then and it won't work now!'

He sprung up out of his chair. 'You're the one that I want!'

She pulled a face. 'Really? That the best you can do? Pfft! You'd better shape up.'

'Please don't go!'

She hesitated. 'KC and The Sunshine Band … good one.'

'Baby, come back!'

She wrinkled her nose in contemplation. 'Well, that could be bloody anyone. Come on, Izzy. Let's get out of here.'

Although the school holidays put an end to the playground gossip for now, it also put an end to the routine of the school runs. Without them, every day rolled into one. There was nothing to get up for in the mornings. No daily schedule to keep to. Every day just seemed to bring a new benefits form to fill out.

Predictably, no amount of Stella's cash or demands was able to secure bail for Gary. He was deemed too much of a flight risk. And when a strong, assertive knock came at her folks' door one midweek morning, Sharon sensed immediately that it wasn't Norma – although as she craned her neck toward the porch hearing the words *social services*, she wished it bloody had been. *What the hell?!*

Their voices spilled through to the sitting room as Sue showed them in.

'Now, obviously we have a duty to follow up reports as I'm sure you'll understand.'

'Oh, I understand right enough, but I can tell you for nothing, you're wasting your time.'

A plump woman with an ash-blonde crop and a tall, skinny man with salt and pepper hair wearing I.D lanyards around their necks entered the room with a squeak of the sitting room door. 'Hello, there. Are you, Sharon? Parent to Isabel Blewitt?' The woman asked.

'I am, yes.'

She nodded. 'I'm Jo Dixon. This is my colleague, David Nichols. We're from social services and we're following up on concerns reported anonymously to us by a member of the public about Isabel's welfare.'

It wasn't hard to guess who!

Sharon sprung up from the sofa. '*What* concerns?'

'Now, obviously, we can't go into too much detail at this stage. Our objective is to follow safeguarding procedures, so we'll need to speak with Isabel one-to-one, then we'll take a look around and ask you some questions yourself, okay?'

'What? This is ridiculous!'

'We do have a duty of care. I'm sure you understand that.'

Sharon nodded, anger flaring in her chest. 'Yes, of course. I'm glad you're around to do what you do, but you've got to understand, this is a vendetta. It's my mother-in-law. I know it!'

Jo Dixon's shite poker face all but confirmed it. 'As I say, we do need to follow up all reports, so if we could just get started…'

'It's her! I know it's bloody her!' Sharon fumed, pacing the kitchen floor while Izzy was being spoken to upstairs.

'I know, love,' Sue agreed, taking frenzied puffs of her third fag on the trot. 'This has got all the hallmarks of that nasty old cow. All because Gary was denied bail.'

'I know. That's exactly what this is. An eye for an eye. She's lost her son, so I'm to lose my daughter!'

'Well, she can try all she likes! Izzy ain't going nowhere, love. That's the thing about making allegations, you need evidence to back it up. And there ain't the slightest bit! They'll soon find that out for themselves.'

'I've lost everything, Mum. I can't lose Izzy, too. I just … I just don't know how much more of all this

I can...'

Sue pulled her into a vice-like hug, enveloping her in that same comforting smell of one-part White Musk, two parts Benson & Hedges and three parts home. It was a smell that immediately took her back to when she'd fallen off her bike outside the launderette and bashed her knee up a good 'un. When Dean Daniels had dumped her. When she'd flunked her exams – things that had all felt like the end of the world at the time, though she hadn't truly known what that looked like ... till now.

The clatter of the back door opening took them by surprise and Jim sighed heavily inside it. 'By 'eck, what is it *now*?!'

'She's only gone and got social services round the house,' Sue told him in a rasping voice.

He pulled a face at Sharon. 'What the feck yer done that for?'

'Not *her*, bloody Stella! They're upstairs now with our Izzy.'

He yanked off his sandy crocs with brute force and threw them down in a heap. 'Oh no they feckin' don't. Not in my 'ouse!'

Sue pulled away from Sharon. 'Don't go charging up there, Jim. You don't want to give the wrong impression.'

'I'm not bothered me arse about that! They can't just rock up here and...' A light tapping at the kitchen door cut him short. 'Hellooo?' Jo Dixon popped her head around it. Her expression hardened as she observed Jim's big, angry tomato-face. 'Right, well, there does seem to have been some sort of misundersta—'

'Misunderstanding, my arse! This is a fraudulent report! It's bloody harassment!' He motioned toward Sharon. 'As if this poor mare hasn't been through enough already. You wanna have that bloody woman arrested, she's a raving lunatic!'

Sue watched Jim clutching his chest and looked at him with pleading eyes. It had always been dangerous to be wrong when he was right, but he was no spring chicken. Any danger was to his own health these days.

'Sir, please,' David interjected. 'What Jo was about to inform you is that we've had a good chat with Isabel, Jo's looked her over and we're satisfied that there's no cause for concern. We're going to head back now and wrap up the report.'

Sharon's shoulders slumped in relief.

'Hang on a minute, surely there'll be consequences for wasting time and resources like this?' Jim questioned.

'That'll be for us to contend with, sir. We've done everything we need to do here, and we'll be out of your way now.' They sloped off quietly and let themselves out.

'You look like shit, mate,' Trace remarked, placing

a steaming mug atop the crushed crystal coaster resting on the mirrored coffee table. Her entire house was a magpie's wet dream and, since Sharon couldn't face the nosy bastards in Greggs, it had become the alternative venue of choice for their coffee meets.

Sharon let out a deep sigh as she took a long sip of her drink. She was a better person when she was caffeinated, but it didn't seem to be having the usual effect. 'I keep expecting to wake up Trace. For it all to have been a dream. It still doesn't feel real. I just don't know what to do with myself. I'm all at sea. Where do I go from here? Where do I even start?'

Trace looked her up and down. 'Well, for starters, you should get down the hairdressers. Have a change, babe. That's what I did after me and my Colin divorced. It doesn't fix you, but it gives you a lift, ready for the next chapter.'

Sharon traced the impressions her rings had left behind after twenty-two years on her wedding finger. 'Dunno about the next chapter, Trace, I've gotta rip it all up and start again. Rewrite the whole shitting book!'

'Might be a better book.'

Sharon gave a pessimistic shrug. She was in no mood for fighting talk. Sometimes all you want to do is wallow in your own self-pity, and today was one of those days. 'Anyway, it'll be a while before I can afford the hairdressers. Our bank account's been frozen. I've not been able to access a penny.

Had to open a new one. My folks have had to lend me money till my benefit claims are processed,' she revealed, pausing as though mentally counting her losses. 'Tell you what, Trace. You soon get used to having money, you know. Everything it buys you. How d'ya go from having a pot of gold to not having a pot to piss in, eh?'

Trace responded with a noncommittal *hmmmmmm*.

'It's like, one minute we were winning at Monopoly, the next, Gary's in jail and I'm bloody bankrupt! I've come full circle, Trace. I've got nothing left.' Her forlorn expression quickly fell straight as she looked over in her should-be therapist's direction to find her grinning from ear to ear and staring at her phone screen.

Trace flicked one smoky eye toward her and kept the other glued to her phone. 'Hang on a sec, Shaz. Barry's just text me.'

Sharon drew her head back in surprise. 'Oh! You're still seeing him?'

'Not half! I've seen all of him. Every crevice.'

'Jesus.'

Trace licked her shimmery lips, suggestively. 'Yeah, that's what I said when I first saw it.'

'Saw what?'

'His schlong … I'm telling yer, hung like a donkey!'

Sharon shifted uncomfortably in her seat, hoping the big reveal hadn't taken place anywhere near the sofa. 'Oh. Well, it's good that you're happy,

Trace.'

'Honestly, mate. I don't wanna rub it in, but you know when you're *so* sexually satisfied that your entire arse area throbs for hours?'

'Um … no.'

'No, I suppose you wouldn't. Well, anyway, that's how good it is.'

Sharon gave a slow, enlightened nod. The only sort of therapy she was likely to get around here would be sex-therapy, which, right now, would be as pointless as the 'g' in lasagne.

∞ ∞ ∞

'Oooh! I see the Shangri-la's looking for staff,' Sue chirped, thrusting The Advertiser across the kitchen table at breakfast on another damp and overcast midweek morning.

'Sod that!' Sharon sneered, thrusting it straight back. Things might have been bad, but they weren't *that* bad! The Shangri-la was always looking for staff and there was a bloody good reason: it was categorically the worst holiday park in all of Britain – as well as the most ironically-named…

Shangri-la:
Meaning: *A remote, beautiful place where life approaches perfection.*

Reality: *Shithole.*

'Beggars can't be choosers, lass!' Jim's voice emanated from the front room.

'What?! The place is a bloody dive!' she choked, wide-eyed. She might not have been enough for Gary, but she was better than The Shangri-la.

'It's money! Don't be too proud, lass.' Jim didn't have to sell his daughter the idea of getting a job, though. She was no stranger to an honest day's work with the 5 AM starts and late finishes at the B&B. But her name was muck around town. Nobody in their right mind would want a fraudster's wife working for them. She hadn't been convicted of any crime, no. But she'd been found guilty in the court of public opinion; guilty by association.

'Look, love. It'll not be long before the DWP's on your back. They ain't gonna pay you to sit about watching "Tenable," she cautioned. 'Yeah, the place wants a lick of paint ... or maybe even tearing down and completely bloody rebuilding come to that. But with all your experience running the B&B, who knows? You could be just the person they need on board.'

Sharon liked a project. And, indeed, she'd been largely responsible for turning the Driftwood into the sought-after seafront success story it had become, but she wasn't a miracle worker, and that's exactly what the Shangri-La needed. Although, as she was confronted with online reviews like *pubes in the microwave* and *a lot like Parkhurst, only less fun*, she concluded that a can of petrol and a box of matches might be more appropriate.

Still, Sue went on and on, like a bloody sofa sale. 'The season's over in October, love. It's June now. Just look at it as a few months' cash to help you back on your feet. If they're desperate for staff, then it's a guaranteed job which means a quick start. And if it's as bad as they say it is, well, it's only for a few months, isn't it?' she wheedled. 'At least go and give it a look.'

Despite Sharon's protestations to the contrary, she knew it made sense. If it was as much of a hellhole as folk said, then a fraudster's wife should blend in nicely.

She took back the newspaper and skimmed over the ad: *Staff wanted across all departments. Full and part-time contracts. Apply within.* What other choice did she have? She was drowning in the depths of despair with no life jacket. Nobody was coming to save her. She only had herself now. There was nothing else to do. She'd have to make a swim for it.

'Good, God!' Sharon muttered, pulling in through the gates of what seemed to be a near-derelict eighties' time warp and eyeing the welcome sign which, due to several missing letters, now read *Shag-a.*

She continued past the play park where the swings were swingless, the slide was little more than a fixture for the birds to crap on and all that remained of the kiddies' spring riders were the bloody springs!

As she drew up to the reception area and surveyed the weeds and flaking paint among a multitude of *out of order* signs, she wondered why, of all the perfectly decent parks in the resort, anyone would willingly make this shitpit their pick of the draw for a holiday – even though she was considering it for a job. The only thing to assume was that it was dirt cheap, and that the images displayed on the company website were about as true to life as a Kardashian selfie.

She bit her lip, climbed out the car and wandered in through the reception door. It was deserted other than for a short and visibly furious blonde lady who stood tapping her neon orange talons on the front desk, her sunburned shoulders just as angry as the scowl on her face. 'If *you've* come ter complain an' all, you'll be waitin' a long bleedin' time!'

Sharon pressed her lips together and glanced down at the beleaguered carpet; not at all ready to admit that she was here for a job. A bloody job!

The longest five minutes of her life passed with Lobster Lady shaking her head and sighing in thirty-second intervals until one of the office doors swung open abruptly and Great Yarmouth's answer to Channing Tatum breezed through it. All at once, time seemed to stand still. Her pulse quickened. Knees weakened. Stomach did a little backflip – just as it had when she'd seen that solo dance in "Magic Mike" – and all the times she'd covertly watched it on her phone on YouTube under the covers while Gary snored like a boar.

'Halle-bleedin'-lujah!' Lobster Lady boomed with a slow handclap. 'D'ya know how long I've been waitin' 'ere? This place is a fackin' joke!' And that was putting it lightly! Sharon had been poised to walk out until *he* did. But now she was staying.

Lobster Lady started screaming like a banshee about the ants in her chalet. 'They're in the kitchen, they're in the bathroom, they're in the bedrooms, they're in the cupboards, they're in the drawers, they're fackin' everywhere!' She yowled. 'Me old man was 'avin a kip on the sofa yesterday ar'ternoon and one crawled up his bloody nostril! Now, I've paid a lodda wonga for this 'oliday and I'll tell yer one thing I *ain't* doin', I ain't paying ter kip down with six thousand fackin' ants!'

Sharon glanced at the beautiful stranger behind the desk leaning casually on one hip, a hand shielding his chiselled, wincing face. He had a manly sort of beauty about him. She couldn't tell his age just by looking, but he looked as though he was somewhere between his late thirties to early forties. Her gaze ascended to his expensive looking gold watch and, before she knew it, she was discreetly craning her neck in search of a wedding ring. Good, God! It was far too soon into Armageddon for her to be ogling strangers. What the hell was wrong with her?! Anyway, no wedding ring. Not that she could see.

'Look, Mrs Turner,' he began, in a husky voice, 'Dennis is on it like a tramp on market chips. He's armed to the teeth with Nippon and he's 'eadin' ter yer digs as we speak.'

'You've godda be jokin!' she bawled. 'You wanna send 'im down there with Napalm, not bloody Nippon!'

'Leave it to us, sweetheart. We'll get it sorted,' he assured, slinking out from behind the desk, affording Sharon full appreciation of his suave and masculine form cocooned in a sheeny gunmetal suit. It was funny, the place was bordering on derelict, and he was standing in among it all dressed like James Bond!

'Now, in the meantime, why don't yer take yer gorgeous self off to the bar for a well-deserved drink on the 'ouse? Yeah?' he schmoozed.

Sharon watched in amazement as Lobster Lady's wrathful rottweiler exterior melted to giggly Barbara Windsor proportions. 'Hm. Well, aaalllright then. But it had best be sorted by the time I get back, yer 'ear? Otherwise, I'll atta put you over my knee!'

'Loud and clear, Mrs Turner. Loud and clear,' he tittered, leading her off by the arm toward the clubhouse doors. 'Give us a sec, darlin,' he winked over his shoulder, sending an involuntary shiver careering down her spine. Blimey! He did well to get out of that one. This man was slick! A smooth operator. Sharon didn't know him from a hole in the wall – and there were plenty of those in this dump – but what she did know, was that for the last several minutes, for the first time in weeks, she hadn't been thinking about her many problems.

Moments later, he re-appeared with a squeak of the clubhouse door. ''Ello, darlin', Mark Chandler, General manager'.

Sharon shook his hand, melting like a Mr. Whippy in the midday sun as he gave it a firm pump. Whatever magic he had was clearly working on her, too – totally without her say so.

'What can I do for yer, sweetheart?'

'I'm, er ... the job advert.'

'Come again?'

Blushing, she averted her eyes. His overconfidence and perma-smirk unnerved her, such that she found herself unable to maintain eye contact for more than a second because it was causing strange flutters in all sorts of places.

'Your advert in The Advertiser. It says you're looking for staff across all departments?' She managed, eventually.

'Ah! Gotta get that taken down. Good job you reminded me! We've pretty much filled all the positions available I'm afraid, darlin, but what sort er thing was yer lookin' for?'

Sharon stared at the Sealife Centre pamphlets displayed on the desk, barely able to remember her own name as the hypnotising notes of his aftershave expeditiously went to work on her. Killer scent like that could only be Tom Ford!

'Well, I was looking for front-of-house, really. I've got bags of experience, I used to manage a B&B...' She stopped herself before she said too much. This could get awkward.

He sniggered, slightly. 'Not the Driftwood, right?'

Jesus! The news had even reached this no man's land!

She felt herself blush. 'Well ... yes. Funnily enough, that's why I'm looking for work.'

He nodded. Didn't probe any further. 'Well, we could always do with some extra hands behind the bar. How would a bar job grab yer?'

She must've misheard him. 'Wait ... you still want to hire me?'

He flashed a toe-curlingly sexy smile. 'Course. Why not?'

Shore is Nice

Chapter 9

Sharon took a deep breath. It had been easy enough accepting the clutch of notes Sue had quietly slipped her in the kitchen the night before. Easier still, pinging a text to Jade to book in. But not so easy now that she was standing outside the hairdressers. Walking in would be the worst part. Partially pampered heads would turn. Prying eyes would examine her the second the door clattered open.

Well, it was now or never...

The salon chit-chat sunk to nothing, and the stylists' scissors seemed to begin snipping at double speed the second she minced mouse-like through the door. The discomfiture was palpable. Their thoughts audible: *yeesh, it's the fraudster's wife!*

'Hiyyyyaaa! Do you want to come overrrrrr?' came Jade's penetrating put-on customer-voice. She threw Sharon a bone in stopping short at asking her how she'd been and she was glad she didn't have to answer *good thanks, you?* Or similar when everyone knew otherwise.

'What are we doing for you today, then?' she cooed in a syrupy voice as she fumbled with the gown.

Sharon took a good look at the woebegone frump reflecting back in the mirror – *her*, not Jade. In a mere few weeks, she'd gone the same way as the Winter Gardens: crying out for an extensive makeover that would only be possible with lottery funding. It was going to take a bit more than a new hairdo to put her back together, but it was a start. 'I'm after a bit of a change, actually.'

'Yeah? What were you thinking?'

She looked again into the mirror, sending the prying eyes shooting off in different directions. *A whole new bloody identity!* 'Hmmm, I dunno. Something fresh. Trendy.'

'I'll grab the colour chart'.

Suddenly, the focus leapt from the elephant in the room to Sharon's exciting new hair as they sat poring over honeys, caramels, and vanillas: *Blondes*. Allegedly, gentlemen prefer them - not that Sharon was planning on having much to do with the male sex for a good while to come. God, no. This was purely for her. The hole in her self-esteem was as wide as the North Sea!

They settled on Ice Platinum and, as Jade hurried off to mix the pre-lightener, Sharon reclined back into her chair with a glossy magazine that was ninety per cent adverts. Luckily, she wasn't reading it. It was just somewhere to put her eyes so that she didn't have to look at anyone.

'Gorgeous colour!' Jade cooed as, what felt like a lifetime later, she masterfully blew out Sharon's new razor-cut bob with blunt fringe. 'Wow! Yeah! Hmmm!' Sharon beamed, face beginning to ache from all the forced smiling. All she could see was *He-Man* grinning back at her. It would either grow on her or she'd have to grow the bugger out.

Over at the desk, she scotched Jade's attempts to sell her half the shelf in pricey salon products and didn't rebook – not just because she wasn't sure about the new eighties' superhero look, but because she was now a single mum on benefits, and this was a one-off pick-me-up … or it was supposed to be.

Sharon glanced in the window of the florist on the way home and did a double take at her new reflection. So did the leery white van driver who honked his horn as he passed. She'd seldom been *honked* so she wasn't sure how to take it. What did it actually mean? Did he expect her to chase the van down the road screaming *I'll give you my number! CALL MEEEE!*? Still, it put a smile on her face; even though he'd looked like a cyclops.

Sharon had often heard Jim say *you only get one chance to make a first impression*, so even though it was just a part-time bar job in a dive, she still scrubbed up for her induction. Just because The Shangri-La's standards were lower than whale shit, didn't mean hers had to be. Although, if she were to be completely honest, her efforts were in part for Mark Chandler, whom, for some reason, she hadn't stopped thinking about. Her nails were filed and painted a summery coral. Make-up on point and hair ... well, still a lot like *He-Man's.*

'Hello, I'm here for my job induction,' she greeted the young receptionist who did not bother her arse to look up. Sharon could see that she was otherwise heavily engaged on Instagram; #Lazybitch.

Christ. If this was the welcome awaiting holidaymakers when they first arrived, then it wasn't hard to guess what awaited them in their digs. Sharon's heart went out to the poor sods as she pictured them arriving all excited with that *holiday feeling.*

'Induction?' The girl parroted, miles away.

'Yeaaah, I'm meant to be starting in the bar?'

'Bar's through there,' she grunted with a half-arsed arm-flap toward the clubhouse doors, which Sharon read as a clue that nobody was expecting her. She raised a brow in disbelief and shuffled reluctantly toward the doors, pulled one open, and slipped into the dingy, deserted clubhouse. It smelt like dirty cloths, stale beer, and piss, and was deadly silent other than for the whir of the air conditioning and the sound of her shoes sticking to the carpet as she walked. She plodded over to the bar and waited. By the time two minutes of twiddling her thumbs had elapsed to ten, she decided that, as desperate for a job as she was, this was taking the biscuit. Then, just as she turned on her heel to leave, the door squeaked open and a butch-looking woman with a dark grey basin haircut wearing a stripey cleaning tabard huffed and puffed her way inside, dragging Henry the hoover behind her. 'Fack's sake!' she grunted, as Henry became entangled around a chair leg. She gave him a vigorous yank and glanced up on her approach. 'Bar's not open till midday, love.'

'No, I'm here for … a job induction.' The words sounded ridiculous, suddenly.

'Are you mad?' The woman asked Sharon, who had then been asking herself the same thing.

She stared at her curiously. 'D'ya know what I'd do if I was you, darlin'?'

She shrugged back at her, expectantly.

'I'd walk outta that door right there and never bloody come back!' She said, in a manner so fierce, her basin haircut shook. But, given that she wasn't tethered and chained to the place, and nobody appeared to be holding a gun to her head, Sharon quietly wondered what was stopping her from taking her own advice. The woman seemed to have heard her thoughts. 'I'm part er the bloody' furniture, me. Been 'ere since 1987 when it first opened,' she excused. 'It's gone to the dogs since then, though. Changed 'ands more times than a good coin in a brothel! Current owner, Mick Hendry, lives abroad. Don't see 'ide nor 'air of him.' She looked Sharon up and down inquisitively. 'You'd 'ave ter be some kinda desperate ter take a job 'ere, sweed'eart. I ain't one ter pry, but I'm intrigued. I can't think why a pretty girl like you would wanna come an' work at a dump like this.'

This was the moment Sharon should've held her tongue; kept her business private – even though much of it had been splashed across the front pages of the local news. But since this woman had no airs and graces about her, and Sharon felt strangely at ease in her company, her mouth ran away with her. Before she knew it, the total stranger had been told her life story. 'Well, you've been through the mill,' she remarked, openly scratching her crotch under her tabard.

'It's been hell,' Sharon agreed, looking a touch grossed-out.

'Well, it ain't much better here, love. This place is hell on earth! And they do say that when you're going through hell, you should keep going, so if you'll take my advice, you'll turn around and—' She froze, quickly grabbed a rag from the front pocket of her tabard and started buffing the crap out of the table in front of her as the clubhouse doors squeaked open and Mark Chandler breezed in. 'Watcha, Mark!' She panted, 'ain't it lovely, this heatwave what we've been 'avin?'

'Depends if you like it hot, Brenda' he quipped in that gravelly voice of his, looking suave and summery in a white short-sleeved designer shirt teamed with smart grey clementine-checked trousers. Wowzas. Mark Chandler certainly had style! Sharon wasn't used to being around such stylish men. Gary had been a double denim kinda guy.

Brenda mopped her fevered brow with the back of her arm. 'I was just getting acquainted with the new lady.' Sharon wondered how it was that she'd managed to break out in such a sweat just from talking.

'You've changed yer barnet!' Mark noticed, flicking his head toward Sharon's hair. 'Suits you!'

'Thanks. You think so?' She patted it down, cautiously. *Hopefully child-Mark was more of a "Spiderman" kid.*

'Yeah! You could pass for a twenty-year-old.'

Brenda rolled her eyes, but Sharon didn't care if he was just being schmoozey. She was bloody well taking that!

'Here. These are yours,' he said, thrusting a couple of cellophane-wrapped royal blue T-shirts her way. She peered down at the Shangri-La logo complete with exotic palm tree embroidered in yellow on the breast, thankful that it was small enough to be easily hidden with a jacket or such while out in public. Beyond this, she'd have to hope no locals saw her walking in and out of the bloody place. They'd love nothing better than to learn she'd been reduced to pulling pints at the Shangri-la.

'I guessed you were about an eight to ten,' Mark added with a smirk that Sharon missed.

The look on Brenda's face suggested that it had been no lucky guess, and that Mark Chandler had a wealth of experience when it came to the female form. She missed that, too.

He rubbed his hands together in readiness. 'Right. I'll show you about, take your pay details, then we'll look at what shifts you can do and stick you on the rota.'

Sharon followed him toward the bar leaving Brenda still buffing the crap out of that same spot. As she glanced over her shoulder, she noted that the speed of buffing had declined significantly.

'You'll be no stranger to pulling pints, then,' Mark suggested as they walked and talked.

'Nooo. Worked all the bars on King Street twenty years back,' she revealed, trying to prise her eyes from his arse which looked rather nice tucked away in the confines of his smart trousers – certainly nicer than Gary's which had been baggy, shapeless, and always seemed to be hanging out … then there were the smells that came from it!

'Ah. well, you'll be well away, then. It's simple enough. Pumps here, spirits there, bottled lagers and ciders in the fridges. Ambients on the shelves,' he continued, pointing it all out with his manly, tanned arms. He was wasting his time, though.

None of it was going in. 'The bar can get pretty chocka. Especially now we're into peak season,' he warned as she followed him out the back and into the cellar.

She gave an enlightened *ah* as she allowed herself another gander at his marvellous derrière.

Perhaps it was the beginnings of a mid-life crisis, or maybe that her sex life had taken a hike off Britannia Pier, but as he stood explaining the procedure for deliveries from the brewery, Sharon found herself imagining the cellar door jamming and them having nothing else to do but rip each other's clothes off.

∞∞∞

Sharon squinted her eyes in the midday sun as she arrived outside Darling Darlings along the seafront. She'd never been to a cat lounge before and wasn't sure what to expect, but it looked too cool for the nosy bastards in Greggs, which made it the perfect setting for a fraudster's wife to get her caffeine fix. She spotted Trace immediately, sat at a table nursing a swaddled sphynx cat in her arms. *Hmmkay, this is different.*

'Watcha, Shaz!' She beamed, delightedly. 'His name's Maverick. Ain't he lovely?'

Sharon peered down at the straight-faced cat and wondered how it could breathe through the

potent fumes of Trace's *Lady Million.* 'Yeah, he's …
great.'

'He's been sat here and not said a word these last
fifteen minutes.'

Sharon wrinkled her nose, derisively. 'Well, he
ain't likely to, is he?' She unzipped her bag, took
out a metallic silver envelope and slid it across the
table. 'Happy birthday, chick. Sorry, present's to
follow. I'll get you something when I get my first
wage.'

'Don't be daft, you ain't gotta get me anything.'

'No, I want to, honest.'

Trace waved her hand dismissively.

'Will you be doing anything nice tonight?'
Sharon asked, instantly regretting the question
when it heralded more explicit Barry-talk. She hid
behind the menu as Trace revealed her secret to
screaming orgasms.

'You've gotta hold off a while, you know? I liken
it to having a good poo, meself. The best ones
are always the ones you've been holding in.' She
then went on to reveal that Barry had been duly
nicknamed *Goldfinger.* 'Because he's so good with
his hands, know what I mean?'

'Yeah. I kind of worked that one out for meself,
Trace.'

Somewhat behindhand, Trace recalled that her
friend was going through a divorce and changed
the subject. 'When d'ya start at the Shangri-la,
then?'

'First shift's tomorrow night.'

'You don't sound too keen,' she remarked, rocking her bundle of cat.

Sharon looked up in dismay. 'Would *you* be?'

'What, with Mark Chandler as me boss? You'd not get me in there quick enough, mate. I'd take a job wiping arses if it meant working with him.'

Sharon tried to keep a poker face, but it was hard when all she could see in her mind's eye was Mark's magnificent behind.

The cat very nearly jumped out of its hairless skin as, putting two and two together, Trace roared with glee. 'You bloody fancy him!'

Sharon felt her cheeks colour. 'No?'

'Yes, you do. You fancy the arse off him!'

'No, I bloody well do not!'

Trace released a knowing huff. 'Listen, this is *me* you're talking to. I've known that look since we was in high school. And I don't blame yer. Mark Chandler's the baddest in town. I tell yer, if he was on me bus, I wouldn't be buying a single, I'd be getting meself an annual saver!'

From his good hair and arresting face down to the tips of his trendy loafers, Mark was knockout. Trace knew it. Sharon knew it. *Everyone* knew it. But nobody knew it more than he did.

Sharon shook her head incredulously. 'Don't talk wet. He's probably dating some model-type twenty years his junior. He ain't gonna be interested in me and I ain't interested in him.' At least not beyond ogling him to death while his back was turned, anyway.

'Well, I wouldn't be too quick to pooh-pooh it, Shaz. You're hot stuff! You've never looked your age. You've a pretty face, nice figure…'

'I ain't looking though, Trace. I've had enough of men to last me a lifetime. All I care about now is building some kind of life for me and Izzy. From now on, it's just me and my girl,' Sharon's tone was firm and resolute. She meant every word.

On Board

Chapter 10

'It's only temporary,' Sharon chanted self-soothingly as she turned in to the entrance gate of the Shangri-la. 'We don't build pyramids from the top; we start at the bottom and work our way up.' It was, as ever, sound advice from Jim. But as she arrived in the carpark and spotted the queue of pissed-off looking holiday makers spilling out of the reception door, she felt like downing tools and forgetting the sodding pyramid! She skidded to a halt in a moment's hesitation. Surely, she could do better than this? Quickly drawing a blank, she moved the car on, parking up alongside a visibly rocking silver people carrier with one of those jokey rear stickers that read *go ahead, hit me. I need the money.* As she switched off the ignition, she would learn that it wasn't a joke.

'I told yer not ter blow all the 'oliday kitty on that fackin' fruit machine!' An angry, muffled screech erupted from the woman sat in the front passenger seat. There were two young lads sitting in the back having a full-on, unencumbered scrap.

'I ain't blown it all. There's still some left!' The driver yelled back in his defence.

''Ow much?'

'About fifty quid.'

'Fifty quid? Fifty fackin' quid? Youuu stupid, bloody arsewipe!' She bawled, raining angry slaps down on him which only made the car rock even more.

Sharon raised a brow and unclipped her seatbelt, just as Mark Chandler, with his suit jacket slung casually over his shoulder, swaggered out of reception like John Travolta in "Saturday Night Fever." She watched in astonishment as he sauntered toward his car – a black Audi TT – which, with its sleek, edgy lines, was just as good-looking as he was. He threw on some shades and roared out of the carpark as chaos ensued all around. Rickety pedal go-karts almost ran down a topless, jaywalking grandad. A toddler throwing a wobbler was being carried off in a fireman's lift. Kids screamed, amusement arcade machines freaked out and, buried somewhere in among it all, was the amplified robotic mutterings of a bingo caller with less charisma than a stick of rock.

Sharon manoeuvred her way through the madness in reception, very nearly mown down herself along the way by two giggling tearaways who were biffing everyone in their path with their giant inflatable hammers. Moments later, the clubhouse doors almost swung off their hinges and an incandescent, scary-looking woman bursting out of a lycra vest and denim skirt ploughed through them. 'LIAM! TROY! GED 'ERE BEFORE I SMACK YER ARSES!'

Crikey, this was a first: holidaymakers who looked like they needed to get away!

Sharon made her way through the clubhouse, which was now a sea of hyper kids, their lips stained blue from Slush Puppy overkill and their neon necklaces luminescing as they ran around like blue-arsed flies ignoring the ents team who were throwing cheesy shapes to "I Am the Music Man".

'You must be Sharon,' a big bloke – whom, with this bald nut, beard and piercings looked a bit like a pirate – greeted her at the bar. 'I'm Steve, bars manager'.

Sharon shook his hand. 'Hello. Nice to meet you'.

'This is Kelly,' he added, nodding toward a younger woman slumped against the back of the bar with her dyed red hair in the sort of high ponytail that gives you an alien-eyed face lift. Kelly teamed the half-smile she made in Sharon's direction with a lethargic wave.

'And this is Jeanette,' he added, flicking his head toward a narky-looking older woman with square-rimmed glasses and a frizzy grey bob.

'Hello,' Sharon greeted her politely as she skulked through the bar hatch with a tray full of dirty glasses.

Silence – save for a stony-faced, non-committal

grunt on her way past.

Sharon cut her some slack. Morale was low. Nobody wanted to be there – guests included. But before too long into her shift, she'd assimilated that they could've all been wearing grass skirts in the Caribbean and Jeanette would still have had a face like a smacked arse. In fact, within a few minutes Sharon had her sussed: she was another Dawn Turner. One of these people who've always wanted to *be* something but never managed it, so they end up bitter little Hitlers, picking holes in everything and everyone. They were only pulling pints, but the way Jeanette carried on, you would think they were performing life-saving heart surgery. Sharon couldn't even slice a lemon without her sticking her oar in.

'Half-moon slices. Yer wanna cut em in half-moon slices!' She yiped over her shoulder with a face like she'd just sucked a truck load of them.

'These *are* half-moon slices.'

'No, they ain't. They're wedges! Keep cuttin' em that thick and we'll soon need our own bleedin' lemon tree!'

Sod your lemon tree! This place wants pulling down!

As the bar got busier, there was no time to dwell on the daft bint.

''Ere y'are!' boomed a voice to her left.

'Nah, mate. I were next!' came another to her right.

The clearly parched pair engaged in a territorial

stand-off, until one of them relented with a disgruntled headshake.

No sooner had Sharon sent them both packing with trays overloaded with booze, than a flurry of sunburned arms shot up. Christ, they were like bloody vultures! It was a totally different vibe to the B&B. *Mind you, what else do the poor buggers have for entertainment?* Sharon thought to herself as the karaoke got underway and some ferrety-looking berk who fancied himself as a Bee Gee wrecked the mic with his tone-deaf rendition of "Stayin' Alive".

Sharon had been about to take her tea break, but she hung around to see how he'd manage that prolonged final note of the Chorus...

'Ah, ha, ha, ha, stayin' aliiiiiiiiiiiiiiiiiiiiiiiiii—' Just as expected, he ran out of breath within seconds and entered into a mad coughing fit. It went on and on, till one of the ents team rushed on stage with some water and stood patting his back while the naff backing track with its robotic backing harmonies played on. Then he picked up where he left off and, suddenly, there was a queue the length of the bar and the orders for vodka went through the roof. Sometimes, getting pissed is all there is, and this was certainly true at the Shangri-la.

Having survived her first shift without walking

out and/or kicking Jeanette, Sharon got in a little after one o' clock in the morning. For a moment – or at least until she remembered that she wasn't doing this for recreation – it felt a bit like the good old days when she'd sneak in rat-arsed during the small hours, spend an age trying to work out which of the three fuzzy visions of front door keys she was seeing was the actual key, slide it successfully into one of three front door locks, then get up to bed without smashing pictures off the walls and knocking shit over. If she could make it upstairs without hearing the tell-tale bed springs that signalled Jim was stirring and, if her liver held out, her worries were light. Now here she was, over two decades on, creeping like a crook into that same darkened front porch with the same old aroma of stale fags and frugality – only this time she was sober as a judge with the weight of the world on her shoulders.

She tiptoed upstairs, de-clothed and fell into bed, observing Izzy's bed opposite in which she was sound asleep, enshrouded by her cuddly toy collection. Suddenly, reality hit hard. Izzy had gone from having her own double-sized bedroom overlooking the sea to sharing the box room at her grandparents' house with her mum. She didn't want this for her girl. She wanted what they'd had. Wanted it all back, but for it to be rightly theirs. This wasn't how it was supposed to be. They'd found themselves in uncharted waters. Now it was down to Sharon to navigate them through without a map.

'Get that feckin' light out!' Jim's muffled bawl suddenly reverberated along the landing in another wave of nostalgia.

Being back home was so bizarre. There were shadows of the past at every turn and ghosts around every corner.

As she clicked off the old-fashioned, fringed bedside lamp and lay alone in the darkness with only her ringing ears and racing thoughts for company, Sharon tried to imagine where they'd be six months from now. She thought long and hard, trying to picture something good for them. Something even better than how it had been before. But as she lay staring into space, she couldn't see beyond the moonlit textured walls of the room.

The Saturday morning sunshine streamed through the crack in the curtains enough to wake Sharon before the alarm. She glanced at Izzy's vacated bed and stared numbly at the swirl pattern of the ceiling, gathering her thoughts as the seagulls screamed and the traffic on the street outside passed in slow swooshes. Already, she could think of two benefits to doing the day shift:

1. Jeanette would not be working
2. Mark Chandler would

By the time she'd utilised every second of her three-minute shower before Jim bashed the ceiling with the broom handle, put her face on and ventured downstairs, a third benefit had added itself to the list: Norma was round again, and Sharon had the perfect excuse to skedaddle, just as Jim had done the second the letterbox opened, and Norma's broad Norfolk drawl came hollering through it. He'd often said that the word *beach* was an acronym for *best escape anyone can have,* and it certainly was where Norma was concerned!

'You've got time for some breakfast, surely?' Sue asked, glancing at the sitting room wall clock as Sharon popped her head around the door to say cheerio.

'I'll grab something there.'

'No, love. Stay and eat properly. You had a late one last night.'

Sharon tried not to look in Norma's direction, but she could see the Santa hat in her side-eye view.

'I'm fine, Mum.' Sharon knew Sue's game. She was just worried Norma might 'faint' and wanted an extra pair of hands to help lift her when it happened.

The tail end of the morning cloud was lifting as Sharon rolled through the entrance gate of the Shangri-la, feeling as though she'd never left.

The park was much more subdued with reception largely deserted – possibly because all the guests were nursing hangovers.

She scanned the carpark for Mark's car which was nowhere to be seen. He was probably still tangled up in some leggy knockout on crisp, white sheets somewhere.

With mostly Brenda the cleaner for company and, as ever, more talking than cleaning happening, in the first ten minutes alone she'd learned that Kelly was *like a doorknob: everyone's had a turn*. Jeanette was *on Tinder*. Lindsay on the ents team was *having it away with the married keyboard player in the resident band*. Brummy Dave from the arcade had *got the park mascot pregnant* – not the actual costume. Dennis the maintenance man was a *pervy old goat*. Steve the bars manager was being paid to *eat crisps and watch porn out the back*, and Mark Chandler *makes Hugh Hefner look like a monk*.

Suddenly, Sharon didn't feel so bad about the Punch and Judy show her life had become; she was in good company.

Later, as she stood buffing the beer taps, a bespectacled chap with a beer gut and mostly grey pattern baldness moseyed over to the bar. Drinking her in through his creepy stare the whole time, he dug inside one of the pockets of his grubby green overalls, took something from it and held his hand out across the bar. 'Fancy a screw?'

Sharon looked down into the palm of his dirty hand and saw an old screw which was about as rusty as his crap chat-up line. She jumped in surprise as he burst into hysterical laughter, baring his God-awful teeth which looked like a row of badly parked Volvos. No introductions were needed for Sharon to know that she was looking at Dennis the Maintenance Man.

Eventually, he calmed himself. 'Ain't seen you round 'ere before, you new?'

She gave a polite smile. 'That's right.'

Following an enlightened nod, he stood looking her up and down, his eyes coming to rest at boob level.

Rather than ask if he'd like a photograph, she asked if he'd like a drink.

He shook his head, his eyes still firmly fixated on her chest. 'Nah, best get back to the grind'.

Sharon's toes curled in her Skechers pumps when he didn't budge. In fact, two or three minutes passed, and he was still standing there, mute as a fish. If it hadn't been for the call that came through on his radio, the git may very well have been there till closing time.

A few minutes later, Sharon had been bent over re-filling the fridges when a cheeky wolf whistle came from behind. She sighed, deeply. Surely, the old bastard didn't think he was in with a chance? Spinning around, her heart lurched as the whistler's identification was revealed, not as Dennis the maintenance man, but as Mark

Chandler; scrummy Mark Chandler, standing at the bar looking dreamy in a black, close-fitting, short-sleeved shirt. 'Alright, blondie? How'd you get on last night?'

She sprung up like a jack-in-the-box from her position by the fridge. 'Er, yeah ... fine, thanks.'

He flashed his winning smile. 'Nothing to it, is there?'

'No ... no, there isn't.' Sharon didn't know where to look as an awkward silence ensued. One thing was for sure, she couldn't look at him for too long. Those eyes! She could easily have lost herself in them.

'So, what's the score then, Sharon? You know, with your old man.'

Her face flushed. *OMG, he's checking to see if I'm available!* 'We're getting a quickie divorce,' she blurted, energetically, before she could stop herself.

He gave a soft chuckle. 'No, I meant do they know what sort of sentence he's looking at?'

Ah, Shit! Sharon felt herself blush. 'Well, he's in custody till the trial. They reckon he'll most likely do ten years.'

He whistled, taken aback. 'Jeez. Ten in the pen.'

'Well, it's not enough if you ask me. All the damage he's done.'

He nodded. 'It can't have been easy for you.'

No, but give us a kiss and I could forget it all in an instant ... SHARON! You're a mother, stop this!

'Well, keep yer chin up, babe,' he said, pulling

down his Ray Ban's from atop his head as he turned to leave. 'Oh, and er … if you get lonely…' he made a suggestible clicking sound with his mouth and swept out of the clubhouse, leaving it on a cliff-hanger.

Sharon pretended she hadn't heard as she turned back to continue filling the fridge, but she'd heard alright. That was a come-on and no mistake! And though she had no intention of getting romantically involved with anybody anytime soon, she couldn't stop smiling.

'There's some post for yer,' Jim announced, gruffly, from his armchair as Sharon arrived in from work. 'I've put it on't kitchen table … with all't rest you've not opened.'

Her heart sunk; back to reality. Moping into the kitchen, she slung her bag and keys down onto the table, pulled up a chair and stared gloomily at the crop of letters all stacked in a neat pile awaiting her attention. There had been a new formula for opening mail since she'd become a skint single mum: brown envelopes were benefits-related and thus, okay to open, white windowed envelopes were bills and thus, could fuck right off. It had been a good formula for a little while … just till she got her head together.

'Don't run away from your problems, lass. It's a race you'll not win,' Jim's voice emanated from the sitting room.

Who's he nicked that one from? Sharon wondered. Though he was right, as ever.

She slid the first letter from the pile, flipped it over and tore it open. It was one of several demands for payment from suppliers that hadn't been paid for their goods and services.

As she sifted through letter after letter, distant echoes of Gary's voice replayed in her head: *we ain't gonna get credit in my name, baby. You've got a better rating than me. We'll have ter put it all in your name.*

She hadn't batted an eyelid at the time. Why would she? This was her husband of twenty years, not some lothario twenty years her junior she'd met on holiday. They were in it together for the long haul. Life partners. When she'd merrily signed her life away on the dotted line, she could never have imagined that she would be doing it for real.

Nearing closer to the bottom of the pile, she felt herself go hot all over as she opened one from the car finance company. *Shit!* They were giving her notice of their intention to repossess the car on 21st July which was in two days' time. Prior to that was the termination notice. And a default notice. Damn! If she'd opened the mail, there would have been time to come to an arrangement with them. Still, realistically, she couldn't afford any amount of money. The car would have to go, but it wouldn't be the end of the world. She'd just walk and get the bus everywhere from now on.

Hook, line and sinker

Chapter 11

With the car now gone, Sharon quickly realised that there was one element to 'just walking and getting the bus everywhere' that wasn't going to work: getting home from work at half-past midnight!

It was Friday night and she'd spent the week trying to prise Izzy away from her iPad and get her out into the sunshine. It was crazy how an ice cream here and a McDonalds there zapped at the funds. One minute, she'd had enough to make it to payday, the next, she was down to her last score. And now, as she stood in the kitchen having desperately checked every compartment in her handbag for a tenner which she might've absentmindedly misplaced, she knew there was only one person who could help her out of this mare's nest.

Sue's head was buried in her copy of *Take a Break* and her motherly sixth sense on aeroplane mode as she lost herself in scandal and heartbreak on the sofa. You'd think she'd had enough of that to last her a bloody lifetime lately, but no. She was staring hard through her purple Poundland reading glasses, emitting enlightened grunts now and then; oblivious to the little coughs in the kitchen doorway that meant her daughter needed to borrow a tenner. There was still a week to go till she was paid and Jim, who's hefty hide was ensconced in the armchair reading the newspaper with his stubby caveman feet resting up on the coffee table, would only give her the third degree about not managing her finances properly. He had no idea as to the true extent of the debts she'd been lumbered with. If he had, he wouldn't sleep at night. Jim Taylor was so tight, he only breathed in. Owing money was the only thing in life that terrified him.

Sharon stood in the kitchen doorway and tried one last cough. If she didn't leave now, she'd be late.

Sod it. I'll cadge a lift home with Kelly. 'You be good for Nan and Grandad, Izzy, okay? Love you, bye.'

With the tail end of the day's sun warming her back, Sharon set off down the street for work. It was a twenty-minute walk to the Shangri-la from Northgate Street, which soon passed as she thought of Mark Chandler every step of the way. What was this strange hold he had over her? What sorcery was this? Why, when there were so many other important things in her life to be contending with, was he the only thing she could think about lately? The question went unanswered as she arrived at the entrance gate which he was then passing through. His car ground to a stop and he put down the passenger window. 'Alright, Blondie? Where's yer car?' His voice was cheery, his smile beguiling.

'I, um … in the garage,' she lied.

'You should've said, I could've picked you up.'

No chance! There was no way she could be in such a confined space with him. She didn't trust him … or herself, for that matter.

'How are you getting home?' He asked.

'I'll grab a lift with Kelly.'

'She's phoned in sick,' he enlightened her.

Shit! Oh, shit! She gave a cool, yet inwardly anxious shrug. 'Ah, well. I'll most probably cadge a lift with someone else.'

He flashed a smile that made her shiver. 'See ya later, then.'

Though it hadn't taken Sharon long to establish that Brenda the Cleaner was prone to chatting shit, she'd been spot-on about Steve the Bars Manager, whose attendance in the building was confirmed by the loud crisp crunching and muffled, disembodied cries of pleasure emanating from the office out back. Sharon shook her head in disgust as she hung her bag and jacket on the coat pegs in the corridor. This was her second week working here, and in that time, she hadn't seen Steve do any work. 'How does he get away with that?' She asked

Jeanette, flicking her head in the direction of the office as she re-entered the bar.

'Dunno. Ain't my problem!' She snapped, slinging a tea towel over her shoulder which Sharon had soon learned was her favourite prop to make her appear busier than she was.

Sour-faced old cow!

'Anyway, he'll atta get his arse out here and give us a hand soon. Kelly's phoned in sick again,' she added over the din of the music.

Sharon's face dropped. *Oh, yeah. Shit! How will I get home?* The thought soon evaporated from her mind as Ollie from the ents team flounced up to the bar singing an impromptu rendition of One Direction's "What Makes You Beautiful". 'Pint of Coke, please. No ice,' he chirped, slapping both hands down on the bar and peering around to see who was looking at him – which was nobody. Ollie never said hello like a normal person. Instead, he would sing in people's faces and wait for them to tell him how great he was. He often had a long wait.

Sharon made pleasant small talk as she fixed his drink. She could tell by the way he stared in every direction but hers that he wasn't listening to a word she was saying. He just kept turning the conversation back to himself and, if she *did* manage to get a word in edgeways, his eyes would begin to dart erratically from side to side as though he might spontaneously combust if he was prevented from talking about himself for a second longer.

Much to the chagrin of Ollie, something happened moments later that took the spotlight.

'There's nobody at reception and I've got a problem I need to report about me chalet.' Sharon looked up to see a hard-faced ginger lady with a jawline that disappeared straight into her neck, standing hands-on-hips at the bar.

'Well, go back when there *is*, then,' Jeanette muttered, rudely.

'I beg your pardon?!'

'We pull pints here, sweedheart! So, unless you want a drink, there's nothing we can do for yer'.

'So, you're tellin' me that there's nobody whatsoever around here who can help? Where's the manager?'

'Oh, he'll be at home with his feet up in front of "Top Gear" by now.'

The woman stood momentarily speechless. 'Eh? So, nobody in the whole bloody place can help me?'

Jeanette turned to Sharon. 'Catch on quick these lot, don't they?'

Sharon's mouth fell open. Followed by the angry guest's. 'Now listen 'ere, you 'aggered old gobshite! I dunno what your problem is. You're obviously a sad old cow with a chip on yer shoulder. Probably got no fella. But let me tell yer this: an ugly personality ruins a pretty face ... and *you* ain't even pretty, so you're fucked!'

Jeanette's mouth fell open. Followed by Sharon's. 'Oh, I'll get my complaint resolved one way or another,' she continued, 'but you? You'll always be an ugly bugger. Ta-da!' It would've been an awesome takedown had the woman not fallen out of the ugly tree herself … and hit a few branches on the way down.

'Pond scum! Utter pond scum!' Jeanette hollered after her, confidently assured that she would never hear over the music.

She turned back to Sharon. 'Does she think I'm bothered? Do I even look bothered? She's nothin' ter me!'

Less than sixty seconds later, Sharon looked up from the Guinness tap to see a clearly bothered Jeanette perched on a bar stool, crying, as the girls from the ents team ambushed her with tissues, rubbed her back and told her she was amazing. Jeanette was a lot of things, but *amazing* wasn't one of them.

An hour or so later, the lesser-spotted Steve popped his head around the door. 'Sharon, Mark wants to see you in his office.'

She frowned in surprise. 'I thought he'd gone?'

'Well, he's had to come back in. Some woman's gone absolutely banzai on Twitter and Mick Hendry's found out. He's been calling, doing his nut.'

Sharon guessed that it was about the incident with the angry guest at the bar earlier. 'What does he want to see me for? I didn't speak to her, it was Jeanette.'

'He knows. I think he wants your take on what

happened before he speaks to her.'

'Oh.'

Sharon finished up serving her customer; a short, buxom woman with enormous bazookas which were straining beneath her spaghetti-strap vest. 'That'll be £8.75 please, love.'

The woman fished out a tenner from her bra and thrust it into Sharon's hand. 'Cheers, babe.'

Why not just get a bloody purse?! Sharon thought as she felt it's clammy warmth.

Mark's office door was closed, but Sharon could smell him through it as she stood in front of it clawing at her hair. God, she'd never known a man who smelled so good. It was a smell that made her go weak at the knees: clean, spicy, musky, and manly all at once. It made her think thoughts that she shouldn't; made her want to do unspeakable things that were completely out of character. She didn't know why he had such an effect on her, but she did know that he gave her something else to think about. Blotted out her problems.

She cleared her throat and knocked at the door.

'Come in.'

Ugh, that voice!

'Steve said you wanted to see me?'

'Yeah, come on in, Sharon … shut the door.'

She gulped slightly as she did so.

'Don't look so worried!' He laughed.

She stood skittishly before his desk, looking around the office; immediately spying a bottle of whiskey which had been not-so discreetly tucked behind some folders. Was he drinking on the job?

He followed her gaze and gave a chuckle. 'Liquid calm … you need it working here.'

She gave him a playfully disapproving tut.

'Anyway, what went on out there tonight?'

She let out her breath. 'Well, I don't want to tell tales on folk, but to be quite honest, Jeanette's attitude stinks. She started it all. There was no need for her to have been rude like that. If I'd have been spoken to in the way she spoke to that lady tonight, I'd be all over Twitter shouting my mouth off about it an' all.'

Mark nodded. He looked even sexier when he was concentrating. 'Jeanette's got a trap and a half on her,' he agreed, 'but she's reliable. Can't keep the staff these days.'

From what Sharon had observed thus far, they couldn't keep the bloody guests either. And they certainly wouldn't keep them with a venomous old bag like Jeanette at the forefront of their customer experience.

'I'll be having a word,' he added, as though sensing her dismay.

'Anyway, let her and Steve hold the fort for a bit. You've got five minutes to chat, haven't you?'

'Um … suppose. What about?'

He relaxed back into his executive leather chair and laughed. 'Just chat in general, Sharon. How's life?'

She chewed her lip. Life was a bitch. But it was

a beach when she looked at him. Trouble was, the current of lust between them was building to dangerous proportions and she was at serious risk of being swept away. The warning signs were everywhere: *Danger, no swimming!*

'Well, um. I'm getting there,' she managed by way of a response.

'Really? You look like you need a night off from it all.'

She shrugged. A year off was more like it.

He read her perfectly. 'Well, I'm a good listener. Why don't you let me take you out sometime?'

Her heart lurched in her chest. Holy crap! Mark Chandler was asking her out! She quickly shook her head before lust answered for her. 'Thanks for the offer, but I can't. I'm not ... looking for anything like that.'

He smiled coquettishly; nor was he. 'Oh, go on! Doesn't have to mean anything.'

Guaranteed, it wouldn't. Nobody as good-looking as Mark Chandler is single just by chance and Sharon had heard enough through Brenda to know that he was a fly-by-night. No good would come from getting involved with him. Although, just feeling those lips on hers would be off the scale. She'd imagined it a thousand times. If kisses were cars, Gary's was the Ford Fiesta: safe, predictable, gets you there ... eventually. And, though she hadn't kissed Mark Chandler, she didn't have to kiss him to know that his kiss would be the Porsche 911 Turbo S: naught to sixty in 2.4

GEM BURMAN

seconds, dangerous ... but thrilling. Some things, however, are best left to fantasy.

'Thanks all the same,' she said, rising to her feet.

Mark nodded. This one was going to be harder than he'd thought. Oh, but that would make it all the finer a catch when the time came. And it would, of this he was certain. 'Okay, but if you change your mind ...'

She nodded; not because she planned to, but just to be polite. 'I'd better be getting back. They'll be snowed under.'

As she turned to leave, the smile was back; the one she couldn't stop.

Brummy Dave from the arcade, who was waiting outside the door as she opened it, assumed it was for him. 'Alroight Sharon?'

'Not so bad thanks, Dave. Yourself?'

'Can't complain, bab, can't complain.'

Of course, he couldn't. He had a wife *and* a bit of skirt on the side. He was living the dream!

'Bit of alroight, in't she?' He remarked when Sharon was out of earshot.

Mark smiled, suggestively. 'She's on the to-do list, mate. Don't worry about that.'

The rest of Sharon's shift seemed to pass in double-speed, which was usually a good thing, but not tonight because she still had the issue of how she was getting home to contend with. Maybe she could ask one of the chaps from the band? She craned her neck, spying one of them still sat at a table with the dredges of a drink. Yes. She'd ask him.

Quickly, she grabbed her coat and bag and hurried out from behind the bar in time to see him gulp down the last of his drink, rise from his seat and slip away with Lindsay from the ents team. Brenda had been right. *Again.*

Great! Now what do I do?

Steve stayed in a caravan on site, and, even if he didn't, getting in a car with him was as good as bumming a lift with Buffalo Bill. And that grumpy old cow, Jeanette, had already done a disappearing act. Her hardest-working-of-them-all ethic seemed to *do one* at home time when she'd literally run out the door before anyone else. There was nothing for it, she would just have to walk.

As she stepped out of reception into the crisp evening air, Sharon spotted Mark Chandler's Audi still parked in the car park. Strange. Like Jeanette, he was usually out the door the earliest he could get away with. There was no way he was still on site. He'd obviously seen off that *liquid calm* and taken a cab home.

The inky sky was clear and the full moon like a floodlight, beaming its silvery shimmer onto the sleepy town below. The air was stiflingly sauna-like, and Sharon was on high alert as she left the entrance gate and began the twenty-minute trek home. Every rustle was the stalker she hadn't known she'd had, following her, watching her every move. Behind every corner was a mugger, just waiting for an opportunity. And every alley mantled a crazed killer, lying in wait for a victim. Her pulse thrummed in synchrony with her hurried footsteps as a showreel of imagined horror scenes played out in her mind.

Further along the main road, anxiety coursed through her stomach as the growl of a car engine came into earshot behind. It seemed to be slowing as it drew nearer. Slower and slower still until it was kerb-crawling behind her. She turned instinctively, blinded by the xenon headlights. The diamond-cut alloy wheels ground to a stop at the edge of the road and the indicator light flashed through a misty veil of exhaust fumes. The passenger door opened from the inside, and soundtracked by abstract strains of Frankie Goes To Hollywood's "Relax", she sleepwalked toward it. Entranced, she pulled it open and climbed straight in. Nobody could save her from the beast now – least of all herself. She knew she was dead meat. She turned her head toward him as he looked at her with hungry eyes, said nothing, and closed in for the kill.

Fresh off the Boat

Chapter 12

What have I done? Was among the first thoughts to hit as the heap of crumpled clothes beside the bed slowly came into focus in the dim hue of first light. Sharon peered down at the immaculate white bed linen partially covering her nakedness as flashbacks of she and Mark Chandler's sweat-enrobed bodies intertwined within the throes of passion replayed from hours earlier. He'd got her. Had her. Ravished her … and all within the first bloody pay cycle! What kind of a mother was she?

Shit, Izzy!

Flinging back the sheets, she darted out of bed, snatched her clothes, and abandoned ship.

'What the bloody hell are you doing, sneaking around at this time of the morning?' came Jim's gruff Northern drawl from the top of the stairs as Sharon crept in through the front porch.

She peered up in dread at his bulky mass enshrouded in the same burgundy dressing gown he'd owned and worn since Christmas 1995.

'I ...' *Think, quick!* 'I, um ...' *Hurry!* 'The g-girl I was going to get a lift home with was off sick so I ... *Accepted a lift off the general manager and shagged him* ... stayed on site with one of the girls from the ents team in her caravan.'

He glowered back at her, suspiciously while she fought to keep eye contact as though it would prove her innocence beyond all doubt; looking away quickly as X-rated recollections of last night emerged from out of nowhere like porn site pop-ups.

'What?! It was safer than walking home at that hour!' She reasoned.

He gave her that look. The one that told her he wasn't buying it one iota. Jim Taylor's unsurpassable fatherly sixth sense knew perfectly well when there was a bloke involved. 'Just you watch what you're doing, lass. You're vulnerable. Don't let anyone tek yer for a ride.'

She already had ... and it was some ride!

'Right, let me just get meself comfy. Hang on a sec,' said Trace, plumping the pillows of the sofa. She lowered herself onto it, tucking her legs under her sizeable behind, and licked her glossy lips. 'Right, I'm ready. *Spill.*'

Sharon hung her head in shame. She wasn't the

slightest bit proud of what'd happened between her and Mark Chandler last night. It wasn't planned. He was like an email subscription she couldn't unsubscribe from: always popping up, tempting her, enticing her. And last night, he popped up right when she'd felt more alone than ever. She took in a deep breath in preparedness to confess her sins. 'Well, they came and took back the car Friday lunchtime,' she began, 'I knew I couldn't afford the repayments and I thought *that's alright, I'll just walk or get the bus everywhere from now on.*'

Trace nodded, visibly eager to get to the smut.

'But I'd forgotten that there wouldn't be any buses running that late at night. I ain't paid till Friday and I didn't dare ask my folks for the cash for a cab, not after all they've lent me already, so I thought I'd cadge a lift with Kelly, but I didn't find out she'd called in sick till I got to work. After that, there was nobody else to ask and I was kind of screwed.'

Literally!

'Oh, Shaz, yer numpty! Why didn't you ring me? I'd have come and picked you up no matter what time of day or night. That's what mates are for!' Trace scolded.

Aww, bless her. She's such a great mate. 'Seriously? You'd have drove and fetched me at half-past midnight?'

Trace looked thoughtful for a moment. 'Well, now I'm thinking about it, I was actually pretty busy at half-past midnight.'

'Doing what?'

'Having it off at Barry's.'

Sharon gave an unsurprised nod. *Of course!*

'Anyway, carry on,' Trace urged with a wave of her hand.

She cleared her throat. 'Well, I was walking home. About five minutes into the journey, Mark's car pulls up. I get in. He kisses me. We drive back to his, and we sleep together … that's about the shape of it.'

Trace let out a beleaguered groan. 'Sod the sleeping part, tell me what happened when you's were awake!'

Sharon bit her lip. Sex wasn't an easy subject for her to talk about. 'Well, what do you want to know?'

The question heralded a full-on interrogation:

'What position?'

'Him on top.'

'What was his body like?'

'Tanned. Defined.'

'Hairy or mostly hairless?'

Mostly hairless.'

'Was he as big as Barry?'

Sharon curled her lip in contempt. '*What?!*'

'Did he exceed nine inches?!'

'Er, no … thank Christ.'

'And did yer get yer laughing gear around it?'

She gave a slow, embarrassed nod.

'And did he return the favour?'

She covered her face with her hands.

'Good! good! And what did he kiss like? Slow and sensual or mad and bitey?'

'Mad and bitey.'

'Lights on or off?'

'On.'

'How long were you's at it?'

'Abouuut … three quarters of an hour.'

'And did you do what I said? You know, about holding off? Did you have a Screamer?'

Sharon looked down, disappointedly. 'Er, no.'

Trace's delighted expression seemed to fall off a cliff. 'Did you even come at all?!'

Sharon felt as though she was letting her friend down terribly when she said it. 'No.'

'My God, Shaz. You've a bloke like Mark Chandler between yer thighs and you can't even finish the job? *Why?!* Didn't the Aussie kiss get the old coals glowing?'

'No, not at all. I spent the whole time terrified I might fart!'

Trace waved her hand dismissively. 'Ahh, what's a bidda wind?!'

'A *lot*, at point blank range!'

Trace tutted. "I'll tell yer what your trouble is, Shaz. You've been tied down to one pillock yer whole adult life. You need some variety. Get back in the dating game.'

Sharon shook her head vehemently. 'No! I ain't ready to date. And I don't even think that's the issue, anyway.'

Trace blinked at her expectantly as she repositioned herself on the sofa.

'I think it's because he's too good looking.'

She burst out laughing. 'That usually helps!'

'No, honestly, Trace. I can't be myself when he's around. I can't have a giggle 'cos of me witchy laugh, I don't talk much in case I say the wrong thing, when I do talk, I put on a different voice.'

'Different in what way?'

'I dunno … cool, intelligent.'

Trace looked astonished. 'Well, if you don't want him, bloody send him round 'ere!'

Sharon shrugged. 'Mark was just an itch that needed scratching, that's all.'

At least that's how she packaged it to herself.

'Oh! You're looking at houses,' Sue remarked in part-surprise, part-disappointment later that afternoon as she nosed over Sharon's shoulder at the kitchen table. 'We did say that you and Izzy are welcome here as you need. There's no rush, love.'

But there was. As much as Sharon loved her folks, she needed her independence. She was a forty-one-year-old woman and Jim's house rules made her feel fourteen again. Though she hadn't meant for last night to happen, she shouldn't be creeping about at her age.

'No, it's time I found my feet.' Sharon's tone was firm.

'Are you sure you'll be able to afford it though, love?'

'Yeah, Kelly at work reckons I'd get help with the rent and council tax being a single mum. If I'm entitled to it, then it would be daft for us to stay cramped up together here.'

'You're right love. You and Izzy need some stability. A fresh start.'

With Trace on standby for a lift, getting home was one less worry for Sharon as she set off on foot to work the Saturday night shift at the Shangri-la. Facing Mark Chandler now that he knew her in the biblical sense, however, was taking up all her head space. Would she still be able to carry on working there with their little secret between them? Would it even remain a secret? All she could do was hope that he'd be a gentleman about it, put it down to a one-off, spur of the moment thing and keep it to himself. And after that, who knows where things might go? But as Sharon approached reception, she was to learn that Mark Chandler was no gentleman.

A tall young woman with Sandy-blonde waves and legs as long as the Acle straight catwalked out in a pair of red shorts. The lifeguard t-shirt and whistle around her neck illustrated her position. Sharon initiated eye contact to say hello, but the woman looked straight ahead as she hurried past.

With a shrug, she continued through the open reception doors knocking straight into Mark Chandler, who, it would appear, was also in a hurry. 'Oh, er ... s-sorry.'

He dusted himself down, half-smiled and hot-footed it straight out the door without a word. Either he was mortified about last night – unlikely – he was being chased by an angry guest – perfectly plausible – or he was on a promise – surely not?

Frowning, Sharon spun around, looked out across the carpark and discovered it was the latter as she spotted the lifeguard leaning against his car, looking just as bewitched as Sharon herself had been less than twenty-four hours ago ... only younger, and firmer.

She remembered Mark's strength as he'd held her. His arms as they'd enveloped her, made her feel safe. It wasn't love, but it had been the next best thing. Mark had needs, so did she, and that was okay. But she couldn't help but be disappointed that he wasn't the person she'd thought he was. He was no saint, that much was apparent. But when gossip was rife and nobody had wanted to know her, Mark Chandler had been the only one to throw her a lifeline. He hadn't probed. Hadn't judged; just gave her a job without question - at least that's how it had seemed at the time. Looking back now, it was obvious: he saw a bit of skirt and thought *I'll have some of that*.

The bastard!

She watched from inside the reception doorway

as they spun out of the carpark in a spray of gravel and dust, kicking herself inwardly as she stared at the grabber machine outside the arcade, feeling much like one of the stuffed toy prizes heaped inside it. Mark Chandler was the claw. He'd picked her up and dropped her quicker than she could blink. And now he was off to have his whistle blown by the lifeguard.

'Ooh, Sharon, it's a nice little place, this. I reckon you'll be happy here,' Sue enthused, following her daughter down the stairs in her two-bed terrace rental in Southtown. It was clean and cosy with a newly fitted kitchen and bathroom, two decent sized bedrooms and a nice little garden with a patio out back.

Sharon smiled, brightly. 'Fab, isn't it?' What she hadn't yet discovered was that her neighbour on the right was a deranged Rick Astley superfan and she was about to learn "Never Gonna Give You Up" word for word and bar for bar.

Trace had bought a new car and in her typically generous spirit, decided to hold off selling her old one, a purple mini convertible, so that she could loan it to Sharon until the season finished at the Shangri-la or she quit; whichever came first. A few weeks had passed since Sharon had made the grave mistake of sleeping with Mark Chandler. She had no intention of giving up her job, though. She'd moved on and, going by his close association with the lifeguard – or *Leanne with the Legs* as she was known among the male members of staff – he clearly had too.

The load had begun to lighten for Sharon. She'd taken free debt advice and, with the councillor's help, devised a monthly spending budget and arranged affordable repayment plans for Gary's and her debts. This, and the new place gave her the breathing space she'd needed, and, for the first time, it felt like she was getting back on track. The pyramid was coming along nicely, and nothing was going to dim her sunshine ... except perhaps for Rick Astley's dulcet tones which, when heard day-in day day-out, are less *dulcet* more want-to-take-a-sledgehammer-to-the-neighbour's-sound-system, or, given the chance, Astley himself.

'Can I get a pint 'e Carling please, darlin'?' The Scots guy chirped from the other side of the bar. 'An' take yin yerself.'

It was Sunday lunchtime and Sharon hadn't been down to work, but she was covering Kelly, who had phoned in sick again and she was far too knackered to be dismantling strange accents.

'Sorry?'

As he looked at her for a moment, he reminded her of Colin Farrell. 'Huv one on me.'

She flushed. 'Oh. Oh, sorry. I didn't hear.'

'Nay bother.' His voice was weary. He was clearly used to it.

'Well, thanks. I'll have a Coke.'

Sharon set about fixing the drinks. 'So, have you been in town long?'

He shook his head. 'Nah, arrived late Friday night.'

Sharon looked around the bar. 'Are you holidaying alone?'

He shook his head. 'Ma lad's away at the arcade. Thought I'd come and get a pint in the meantime. Cannay stand the rabble 'e they machines, no?'

Sharon nodded, even though she'd only been able to pick out *arcade* and *pint* from all that. What she had deciphered, though, was that there had been no mention of a wife/mother figure holidaying with them.

'What part of Ireland are you from?'

He looked at her gone out. 'I'm no fae Ireland, darlin', I'm Scots. Aberdeenshire.'

Sharon was mortified. 'You'll have to forgive me. Geography was never my thing and I'm no good with accents, as you can probably tell.'

The man laughed and stretched his arm out across the bar. 'I'm Grahame, by the way.' He had a firm handshake.

'Sharon. Nice to meet you.'

'So, Sharon. Whit's there tae do around here? Can ye recommend anywhere fer me and ma lad tae try?' An awkward silence ensued before he repeated the question again, this time more posh-Scottish, like Ewan McGregor.

'Oh, oh, right. Yeah! There's loads to do. How long will you be staying?'

'Ten days. A wee bit longer than a week but doesnay drag like a fortnight, no?'

'Right. Well, you've got the seafront, obviously. That's where all the action is. There's the Pleasure Beach, and if your lad likes the arcades, he's going to have a field day, let me tell you that!'

Grahame feigned a fatigued eyeroll.

'Then there's Quasar, the laser game. I'm guessing your lad would be into that. He sounds like a gamer.'

'Wait … you've a gamer yourself!'

Sharon giggled. 'My daughter, Izzy. She's a bit of a tomboy. Loves all that stuff.'

Grahame took a long sip of his cold beer. 'Really? How old?'

'She's coming up for twelve now.'

'Same as ma boy, Mikey. He'll be twelve in December.'

'Sharon smiled in surprise. 'You've also got crazy golf, The Waterways, the two piers, bowling,' Sharon continued. 'And, if you like a flurry, there's the Racecourse and Yarmouth Stadium if you like greyhound racing.'

'Sounds like it's gunna be a busy ten days!'

Sharon laughed, her witchy laugh. 'I reckon you'll have to swap your beers for Red Bulls.'

Half an hour flew as they chatted about everything from British vs Scottish weather, what haggis is, deep-fried Mars Bars and whether Scots men really do go commando under their kilts. Grahame was adamant they did, though Sharon reasoned that unless he was in the business of lifting men's kilts, how would he really know?

'Can I huv some more dough, Da?' A young lad who was clearly Mikey asked as he sidled up to the bar.

'No! You're no feeding they machines wi' any more 'e ma cash, son. Let's get aff and get some sea air.' Grahame picked up his glass and drained the rest of it.

Sharon glanced at her watch. 'My shift finishes in five minutes. Can I give you boys a lift to the seafront?'

'That'd be grand if we're no putting you oot.'

'Not at all.'

'Nice wee motor you've got there, Sharon,' Graham remarked as she unlocked the car and put down the roof out in the the carpark.

'It's actually a friend's. I'm just borrowing it for a while, but thanks. Jump in!'

It was scorching out, and the steering wheel was red-hot inside the car. It would be a relief to feel some breeze when they got going – although it would make it even bloody harder to hear what

Grahame was saying.

'So, how long have you lived in Yarmouth, Sharon?'

'Born and bred,' she shouted back.

He nodded. 'You like it?'

'Yeah. Some of the other locals might tell you different, but I think we're lucky to have all this on our doorstep, you know? I'd take this over city life any day of the week. I just love being by the sea.' *Christ. I sound more and more like Dad every day!* 'What about you, do you like it up North?'

'Aye, it's alright. No bad at all. I'm no one of these nationalists though, you know? I could live anywhere in the world.'

'And what is it you do? what line of work are you in? ... Sorry! That's really nosy.'

Graham smiled, hospitably. 'Nah. I'm in engineering. Oil and gas. It's no the first time I've stayed in Yarmouth. I've been here with work a few times, actually. I'd always thought about bringing Mikey doon for a wee holiday so ... here we are.'

'Lovely!'

There was still no mention a wife/mother figure, and it didn't feel right to ask.

'Well, here we are!' Sharon announced as they drew up outside Wellington Pier.

'Here ... for your petrol,' Grahame said, flourishing a fiver toward her.

'Don't be daft, it was my pleasure!'

'No, no. Fuel prices are crazy just now. Here, take it,' he nodded toward the petrol gauge and Sharon cringed inwardly as she saw the needle touching red.

He smiled. 'Still cheaper than a taxi!'

'No, honestly…'

Grahame pushed open the ashtray and stuffed the fiver inside. 'Come on noo, Mikey. Let's get aff an' spend some more 'e yer dad's dough.'

Sharon watched from the driver's seat as they clambered out onto the pavement outside.

'Well, cheers Sharon. Good tae meet you,' Grahame chirped, closing the passenger door with a clunk.

'Likewise!' She smiled and gave them a little wave as she drove away. *He was nice,* she thought to herself.

Vitamin Sea

Chapter 13

During the week, Sharon received a call from the police. Gary had decided to plead guilty to all charges against him. The trial was off! It was music to her ears. No trial meant that their lives would no longer be in the public domain. Gary would begin his sentence and she and Izzy could get on with the rest of their lives. But the mark of disgrace from her association with Gary would prove to be hard to erase...

Evening all. Just a heads up, we've had some cash go missing from the tills in the bar. Not pointing fingers. Just asking everyone to take care when giving out change and to be extra vigilant. Cheers. Steve.

Sharon stopped straightening her hair and stared at the text that lit up her phone beside her. Having worked in bars and retail for years, she was used to cash handling and seldom made mistakes on the till. But even so, she was a fraudster's wife. If anyone was pointing the finger, naturally, it would be at her.

As she went in to work to begin the Tuesday evening shift, her suspicions were confirmed within minutes.

'I've worked here the last three years, and, in that time, we've never had money go missing from the tills,' Jeanette swiped as she made a performance of bottling up. Her voice was deliberately elevated and dripping with venom.

As much as she wanted to, Sharon didn't bite as she stood filling the ice buckets.

'Could be a mistake,' Kelly muttered, deeply immersed in her Tinder matches.

'If it were an odd amount, perhaps. But a straight score? Pull the other one!'

Sharon stopped shovelling and sighed deeply. The perpetrator was behind bars, yet she was doing time herself, imprisoned by invisible chains. How was she ever to escape Gary Blewitt and his lousy, rotten deeds? He was a stain on her character. The flake in her 99 problems.

'Do you think we might borrow your glass collector for ten minutes around nine o' clock?' Darren from the ents team asked, sidling up to the bar.

'Whaddya want that lanky drip for?' Jeanette demanded, hands-on-hips.

Darren's eyes widened slightly. 'We've a special guest, lovely old dear. She's just turned ninety today,' he explained. 'We're going to sing happy birthday to her, get her up onstage with a cake. Only, we need the mascot to bring the cake out but

Shanice ain't here. Brummy Dave says she's really suffering with the morning sickness. D'ya reckon Neil would do it for us?'

'He'll be here in fifteen minutes. Ask him yourself. But you can have him all night for all I care. He ain't no use to us. Collects more bloody Pokémon than he collects glasses,' Jeanette scoffed. It was strange that people brought their queries to Jeanette when she had zero authority. But she loved it. You could almost see that frizzy grey bob of hers expanding as her head swelled.

An hour on, Jeanette wasn't so pleased to be looked upon as the boss when a woman covered in tattoos and built like a brick shithouse ambled past the bar, thumbing toward the ladies'. 'Shitter's blocked!'

Her horrid old face settled into an even deeper frown. 'Pardon?'

'Some bugger's had a seismic shit. Blocked it bigtime!'

Jeanette stood shaking her head. 'We've got a code brown, ladies.'

'Well, don't look at me!' Kelly sneered. 'I ain't paid enough for that shit … pun intended.'

Jeanette's steely gaze flipped toward Sharon, who was down to the last reserves of her patience. 'And *I'm* busy serving, Jeanette!'

'Why am I the one that everyone looks to?' Jeanette whined, indignantly.

Because you wouldn't have it any other way, you bossy old cow! Sharon smirked as she skulked off around the back. The thought of Jeanette armed with a plunger and a seismic scowl to match the ordure in the ladies' was making her giggle. She couldn't think of better just desserts.

'Pint 'e Carling when you're ready please, darlin'.' Grahame's voice brought her out of her reverie.

She looked up in surprise, genuinely pleased to see him. 'Oh, hello again!'

He smiled back at her. 'How you doing?'

'Fine. Yourself? How did you and Mikey get on at the seafront?'

'Oh, grand. We hud a whale 'e a time.'

She chewed her lip and giggled.

Grahame rolled his eyes to the ceiling, playfully. 'We. Had. Fun. There! You get that okay?'

She laughed her witchy laugh. 'Where's Mikey?'

'Three guesses.'

'Arcade?'

'Aye, he's away spending ma dough again.'

Sharon threw him a Duchenne smile. He was fun without trying to be.

Darren's sudden announcement over the PA system got everyone's attention. 'Okay ladies and gents, if I could steal your eyes and ears for a minute or two, we have some wonderful news to share.'

'You finally been closed down?!' Someone shouted, invoking torrents of sniggers.

Darren cleared his throat. 'Now, we've a very special guest who's been coming here for years and years.'

'Well, they must be a glutton for punishment!' Another voice boomed from across the room.

Darren closed his eyes in exasperation and quickly recomposed himself. 'And today, she's celebrating her ninetieth birthday. So, ladies and gents, I'd like you all to put your hands together and welcome Elsie to the stage!'

Sharon watched from the bar as the petite, old lady was helped to her feet. Supported by a relative either side, she pootled slowly across the dancefloor to a round of applause and an orchestra of whoops and cheers. A chair was brought onto the stage by one of the girls from the ents team and, having eventually made it up the steps, Elsie shuffled over and lowered herself into it.

The resident band struck up a fanfare and launched into a flamboyant recital of Happy Birthday as Hank the Dog – possibly the strangest-ever-looking cross-eyed mascot – brought out a cake from the side of the stage. Elsie smiled delightedly from her chair as Hank blundered haphazardly toward her, somehow managing to trip over his own feet in the process. Next, in what seemed like slow motion, he nosedived toward Elsie and fell heavily on top of her. The audience stopped singing and gasped collectively as the chair tipped over backwards and both dog and OAP wound up a tangle of legs and cake. A stunned three-second silence ensued before Hank's tail was set alight by the vast array of lit candles. Then, it was all systems go! The ents team made a mad dash to rescue Elsie from under Hank as Darren raced on stage with a fire extinguisher and began erratically hosing Hank's arse.

The entire clubhouse fell silent, every jaw at every table hanging wide open.

Scattered claps followed toward the back of the room.

'Bloody brilliant!'

'Best show yet!'

Grahame turned to face Sharon at the bar. 'Well, there's a birthday she'll nay forget in a hurry.'

With poor old Elsie packed off in an ambulance just to be on the safe side and Neal sent home, Jeanette took it upon herself to delegate glass collecting duties to Sharon, which she didn't mind since it got her out from behind the bar and away from the miserable old bint.

The ents team wound down from the chaos earlier with Ollie singing some slowies for what was left of the audience. Sharon chuckled to herself as he belted out Westlife's "Flying Without Wings", visions of Hank doing just that replaying in her mind.

Next, as he launched into Ed Sheeran's "Thinking Out Loud", she felt a tap on the shoulder. Grahame stood smiling behind her. 'Like a wee dance?'

Sharon smiled hospitably, cautiously scanning the bar for Jeanette. Only Kelly appeared to be serving last orders. The old dragon was obviously on another of her many fag breaks. 'Um, yeah … why not?'

She placed her handful of empty glasses down onto a vacant table and followed him to the dancefloor.

She was cool, calm, and collected as Grahame took her hand in his and drew her gently toward him by the waist. 'So, is it always this crazy here?'

Sharon laughed quietly as they swayed amiably to the music. 'Let's just call tonight a one-off spectacular.'

'Aye, it was some show.'

'Where's Mikey?' She asked, peering around the tables.

'Arcades have closed so he's away back tae the caravan tae play his Nintendo while I finish ma beer.'

She nodded.

'Listen, we didnay manage tae squeeze in the Pleasure Beach on Sunday, so we were planning on going tomorrow. I'll no go on many rides though, which means Mikey would huv tae go on a lot of them on his own. I was wondering, if you're no working, would ye fancy bringing your lassie along wi' us tae make the numbers up?'

She didn't hesitate. 'Sure! I'm not working next until Friday. I'm sure Izzy would love to go.'

He smiled warmly down at her. 'Awesome.'

∞∞∞

Sharon pumped the mascara wand and zig-zagged it through her lashes, staring open-mouthed into the bathroom mirror.

'Why do you have to open your mouth like that?' Izzy's voice came from outside on the landing. 'It doesn't go on your mouth; it goes on your eyes.'

Sharon chuckled. 'Dunno, sweets. But try doing it without, it doesn't go on as well.'

She plodded into the bathroom and sat down on the edge of the bath. 'Why are you getting all dolled up, Mum?'

'I'm not. I always wear make-up.'

Izzy wrinkled her nose, dubiously. 'But you're wearing your pink lipstick. You only wear your pink lipstick on special occasions.'

'Yes, well ... this *is* a special occasion, sort of. We're having a day out with friends.'

'But we don't even know them.'

Sharon held the wand mid-air. 'Don't be silly, Izzy. *I* know them. They're good fun.'

'Yes, but you've only just met them.'

She let out a deep sigh. 'Izzy! We're meeting them at the Pleasure Beach to go on some rides. We're not bloody moving in with them!'

Sharon paused and stared into the mirror as Izzy left again. She had a point; they *had* only just met. But, even so, Grahame had an open, warm friendliness that made him feel like an old friend. Maybe it was a Scots thing. Most Scottish people she'd encountered seemed to be like that. But in any case, she had no qualms about meeting them. It was all very pleasant and natural.

As they stood outside the Pleasure Beach entrance waiting for Grahame and Mikey, Sharon delivered the usual peptalk. 'Now, Izzy. Be polite, okay? No swearing. Make sure your trousers are pulled up properly and don't you be rude when they get here! I want you to be nice to Mikey, okay?'

'I'm not gunna be nice to someone I don't even know.'

Sharon wagged a coral-pink nail at her daughter. 'If you embarrass me, you'll be banned from the iPad for a week!'

Izzy's scowl seemed to evaporate instantly, and just in the nick of time as Grahame and Mikey approached. 'Hey, there!'

'Hey! Lovely day for it, isn't it?'

'Aye, the sun has certainly got his hat on.'

Sharon turned to Izzy, relieved to see her smiling sweetly. *Good! Works every time.* 'Izzy, this is Grahame's boy, Mikey. He's the same age as you.'

Izzy's smile widened. 'Hiya.'

Mikey smiled back, politely. 'Hi.'

Grahame and Sharon exchanged visibly relieved looks now that the introductions were done. 'Right, let's get away inside and check oot the rides.'

The seagulls crooned and the late-August sun beat down in full force as they meandered through the crowds among shrill screams, cheerful carousel melodies and the clickety-clacking of the log flume.

Sharon noticed Grahame's physique as he walked out in front of her. Though he was indeed a father, that was certainly no dadbod. He was tall with broad shoulders showcased in a tight, white t-shirt, a narrow waist, flat stomach, and strong, manly arms. Sharon had a thing about arms, but she was very specific. They mustn't be white, overly hairy, or flabby ... like Gary's, which had been *all* of those things. Still, she hadn't married him for his arms. She'd married for love – or so she'd thought.

'Can we go on the pirate ship, Da?' Mikey asked, tugging Grahame's arm.

'Christ, no, son. I cannay go on that thing. No unless ye wanna see yer poor Da puking all over the place.'

'I'll go on it with you,' Izzy offered, looking at Sharon as if to say *I'm being nice, see? You won't take the iPad, will you, mum?*

'Cooooool!'

Sharon smiled, watching as they ran off to join the queue.

'How about we grab a quick coffee?' Grahame suggested.

She nodded, enthusiastically. *Hmm! A coffee drinker,* she thought to herself. Not that there was anything strange about men drinking coffee, it was just that Gary only ever drank tea, proper builder's tea, so it seemed sort of ... sophisticated.

Sharon liked that.

She followed him to the nearest refreshments stall and allowed herself a discreet assessment of his behind as he turned his back to order. It was okay. Pretty good. Not a patch on Mark Chandler's, but then nobody's was … not even bloody hers! But for what Mark Chandler had been blessed with arse and looks-wise, he significantly lacked in all other areas.

'De ye's do Americano?'

Ooh! Not just a coffee-drinker, he's a connoisseur!

'No, sorry, just regular instant,' the woman behind the counter replied.

'Alright, that'll do fine, ta. And for you, Sharon?'

'Same for me, please.'

He nodded and turned away again.

Sharon noticed that Grahame seemed to have a calm, easy-like-Sunday-morning demeanour. He never seemed hurried or nervy, which was refreshing when the whole world is in a rush.

He handed Sharon a cup of coffee. 'Lovely, cheers.'

'Listen, thanks for coming today, Sharon. It's good tae get him aff they bloody games fer a while, you know what I mean?'

'God, yeah. Story of my life! Izzy's just the same. Game-mad!'

'I try tae take him oot as much as I can, like. But it's difficult around work, ye know?'

Sharon nodded, guessing that Grahame was divorced. 'Does he go out with his mum much?'

His face fell a touch. 'Er … no. Tilly, his ma … she died three year ago from Breast cancer.'

Sharon bit her lip. 'Aww, Grahame. I'm sorry to hear that.'

He nodded. 'Aye, she was only thirty-eight. We've just hud tae find a way tae manage ever since. It was a nightmare to begin with, but we're getting there and days like today … they mean a lot to us, so thank you.' His voice was sombre yet sincere.

'Well, you're doing a great job. Mikey seems like a lovely lad. You guys seem really close.'

'Aye, we are. You kinda become a mum and a dad rolled into one, you know?'

She knew perfectly well.

They sipped their coffees in silence until Sharon cleared her throat. 'Well, Izzy's dad … he's in prison. I'm divorcing him.'

Grahame looked taken aback. He stood and listened; his dark eyes full of empathy. Before she knew it, they'd exchanged backstories.

'Jeez, sounds like it's been some year for you's.'

'Certainly has. I'll be glad to see the back of it.'

'Muuum, we're going on the rollercoaster!' Izzy hollered from ahead, racing off with Mikey.

'Well, they seem to be hitting it off,' Sharon remarked. She tossed her empty cup into the bin and turned back to Grahame. 'Do you fancy it?'

He raised his brows. 'Are ye offering?'

She covered her face with her hand, cringing inwardly. 'I meant the rollercoaster.'

He laughed. 'Is it nice and tame?'

'Tamer than sleep.'

'Aye, alright then. Why not?' They followed Izzy and Mikey to the rollercoaster, only just making it onto the same train.

'God, we're right at the back,' Sharon laughed, climbing into the car first. Unexpectedly, she felt the whole of her left side tingle as Grahame climbed in and sat beside her, his right leg resting closely against hers. He pulled down the safety bar and nodded toward the front where Izzy and Mikey were sat. 'Aye, this is the wrong way aroond. Shouldn't it be old fogies tae the front, daredevils tae the back?'

Sharon thwacked him playfully on the arm. 'Old fogies?! Speak for yourself!'

They laughed jocosely as the train moved off with a loud, squeaky groan. Sharon felt light. Carefree. This was fun. *He* was fun. She couldn't remember the last time she'd felt so at ease … until they began to climb the first hill. 'Ugh, I hate this bit! What if we fall back?'

Grahame looked at her gone out. 'There's a chain pulling it up. And even if the chain packed in, it would just roll back doon along the track. It's no gonna come right aff it, yer wally.'

She squealed, closing her eyes, and grabbing his hand before she knew what she was doing. 'S-sorry … it's just, this thing's as old as Elsie from last night.'

'Is it?'

'Yeah, it's a grade II listed building. Hasn't even got any brakes. See the dude sat there in the middle? That's his job.'

Grahame pulled a face. 'Well, let's hope he's no away wi' the fairies today.'

She laughed. Grahame had a funny way with words.

He turned to look at her. 'Just do me a favour will ye?'

'Yeah, what?'

'Open yer eyes! I've never understood why people pay ter go on rides just tae sit wi' their eyes closed. If ye keep yer eyes closed ye miss all the fun!'

Sharon opened one eye. 'How's that for a compromise?'

The train reached the peak of its ascent and plunged down the first hill, dragging the back carriages along fastest behind it.

'I see what ye mean aboot it being tame as sleep,' Grahame laughed.

'Well, I didn't bank on us sitting right at the back,' Sharon warned, 'let's reserve all judgement till after the Headchopper.'

'What's that?'

Sharon squeezed his hand even tighter. 'THIS!'

The train rattled along the last of the circle of track, dramatically picking up speed before plunging down the next hill, the steepest plunge of the lot.

Their stomachs dropped. 'Jesus Christ, it's a

good job ma hair's ma own!'

It was funny. Sharon had ridden the rollercoaster incalculable times, had lived here all her life, and yet here she was, having more fun than the holidaymakers.

When the train rolled to a stop in the station, Sharon realised she was still holding Grahame's hand. Though he didn't seem to mind, she felt suddenly embarrassed and quickly drew it away. 'How about the snails, now? Bring the blood pressure down a bit?'

'Sure!' Grahame held his hand out to help Sharon out of the car. She took it once more and felt her fingers tingle as her skin met with his again. What was this sudden chemistry? Could he feel it too?

'Mikey! Head fe' the snails, son,' Grahame hollered after him as he and Izzy pegged it down the steps. 'Where the hell do they get their energy at that age?'

Sharon smiled, pleased that they were getting along. 'Beats me.'

'I've no been on the snails since I was a bairn!' Graham said, as they climbed into the car.

'A what?'

Grahame dropped his head, wearily. 'A kid!'

'Ah! Me neither. Felt like a waste of a token back in the day when you had all the white-knuckle stuff to get through. They're a lot cooler these days, though.'

The car moved off with a jolt and Sharon squealed as it took her by surprise.

Grahame shook his head in dismay. 'Dinnay tell me you're gunna need ma hand again fe the bloody snails?'

They yattered away like old friends as the car clickety-clacked along the track, whirring through the tunnel and back out the other side.

Grahame fell quiet. 'I know it sounds daft, Sharon, but I feel like I've known ye years ... all ma life, in fact.' His voice was low and reflective.

She gasped, quietly. 'D'ya know what? I was thinking the same.'

'You were?' He seemed surprised and relieved all at once.

'Yeah, it's like we've known each other...'

'In another life or something.' Whoa! Now he was even finishing her sentences for her. Though it didn't make any sense, the sense of déjà vu between them was palpable.

Sharon didn't know what else to say as the car whirred into the next tunnel. Fortunately, the explosion of The Sherman Brothers' "It's a Small World" filled the silence nicely, and, as the car continued on, both quietly recognised the significance of the lyrics in that moment.

Life's a Beach

Chapter 14

When Sharon had invited Grahame and Mikey over for dinner with she and Izzy the following night, she hadn't given thought to the deranged Rick Astley superfan next door. What would Grahame think? Would he even be able to *hear* himself think over those Stock Aitken Waterman beats? Well, it was too late now, they would be on the way over in a cab. The spaghetti Bolognese was simmering away on the hob, and she'd splashed out on a bottle of Tesco Finest Barolo Docg ... Christ only knew how you pronounced the bugger, all she knew was that it was Italian, so it ought to complement the grub nicely. Sharon smoothed down her Bardot floral maxi dress and gave her platinum beachy waves a zhoosh. She'd caught the sun yesterday and her shoulders were nicely browned; her face freckled and golden. She was glowing – but it was mostly from within. She had no idea where any of this was going, but the butterflies in her stomach told her that she couldn't wait to see him, lovely Grahame.

The doorbell rang around ten minutes later, and she was relieved to hear silence from next door. Perhaps they'd gone out for the evening?

'Wow!' Grahame remarked as the door opened back. 'You look ...'

Mikey peered up at his dad with raised brows and Grahame looked down at his son, sheepishly.

'... nice.'

'Thanks, so do you,' Sharon giggled, showing them in. And he did. In fact, he looked even more handsome than she'd remembered. How had it escaped her notice the first time they met? She wasn't sure.

When she'd opted for Spaghetti Bolognese, a good all-rounder that most people like, it hadn't crossed Sharon's mind that it's one of the most difficult meals to eat elegantly and, thus, usually ought to be avoided at all costs ... unless one is deliberately going for a "Lady and The Tramp" moment. But strangely, as she shovelled away forkfuls of spaghetti at the kitchen table, she didn't seem to care, and nor did he. They ate as if they ate together every day.

The kitchen was silent, but the silence was easy.

'This is really good, Sharon,' Grahame said, eventually.

'Aww, thanks. There's Eton Mess for afters so leave some room.'

Izzy and Mikey disappeared off to the sitting room

to lose themselves in Minecraft as Sharon and Grahame co-jointly cleared away the dishes and tackled the washing up.

'I'll wash, you dry,' Grahame suggested. His strong, soapy hands made light work of scrubbing the pans. Sharon couldn't recall having ever seen Gary wash up so much as a mug in all the years she'd wasted on him. It was just another aspect to Grahame that was endearing to her.

'It's still warm out. Shall we have our drinks out on the patio?' Sharon suggested, smiling as Grahame wiped down the kitchen counter till it was spotless.

'Aye, go for it.'

The balmy evening air hit as Sharon slid back the patio door and set the bottle of red and two wine glasses down onto the table outside. She pulled up a chair and smiled contentedly as Grahame poured out the drinks.

They chinked glasses. 'Cheers'.

Sharon gazed at him over the rim of her glass and felt herself falling. She could get used to this. To him. To the way she felt when she was with him: a feeling that time had stood still. It was only them. The sky could be falling down, and she wouldn't have noticed.

Before either of them could speak, there came the dreaded eighties keyboard drum intro, and same explosion of strings she'd heard non-stop since move-in day ... bloody Rick Astley again!

Sharon's head slumped wearily onto the patio

table.

Grahame chuckled. 'Take it you're no a Rick Astley fan?'

'You don't understand. It gets played on the hour, every bloody hour!'

'Seriously?'

She gave a confirmatory exasperated nod and watched in disbelief as his shoulders started to go and he clicked his fingers. He laughed. 'It's a classic. Ye cannay beat it!' She looked on as he sprang up from his chair, pulled her out of hers and twirled her around on the patio. She was stiff and unwilling at first, but by the first chorus, she'd loosened up and the pair of them were singing out of tune and throwing shapes together. Anyone watching would have assumed they were pissed, but, for the first time in a long time, Sharon was thoroughly high on life.

Fast forward an hour and the vibe was decidedly less high as they sat at the table with their heads resting glumly on their hands while Rick played on … and on … and bloody on. It was hard to think over the din, but both had a thousand things they wanted to say.

Grahame pulled his chair closer to hers until the chair legs were touching. They looked at each other and smiled, but each held back from speaking, as though doing so might spoil the moment; a moment best left without words. As Mozart once said *the music is not in the notes but in the silence between*. They hung on, until the tension hit fever pitch, then, finally, Grahame leaned across, took her face in his hands, and kissed her: soft, slow, and deep. There was nothing to compare to it. It was electric. No man had ever kissed her like that. She seemed to float away on a cloud as he ran his fingers through her hair. It was just the two of them, connected, lost in the moment under the stars. She could've quite easily kissed him forever.

'I ... dinnay normally do that,' he said, his voice low and reflective as they came up for air. 'It's the first ... it's the first time. You know, since Tilly.'

Sharon had been poised to agree that she too didn't normally do things like that ... till she remembered the mad sex with Mark Chandler weeks before. But that was all it had been; sex. Animalistic. Meaningless. This was different. She couldn't put her finger on it, but it just felt right, as though it needed no excuses.

'Da, I'm out of charge on my phone,' Mikey's voice came from the patio door.

Grahame sat bolt upright and quickly pulled his chair away. 'Okay, son. We probably ought tae be heading back tae the camp now, anyway. It's getting late.'

Sharon's heart sank. She didn't want him to go. He felt like Christmas times twenty. She knew that, were it not for the kids, he would be staying the night and, going on that kiss – one that would live forever rent-free in her mind – she was in no doubt as to the sort of experience it would be. Now she'd had a taster of what she'd been missing all this time.

Grahame called a cab, then got up from the table. His posture was reluctant. 'Well, thank you, Sharon. Dinner was grand, it's been lovely.'

'My pleasure.' She followed him through to the sitting room, still on fire from that kiss. Neither of them needed to say it. They were repressing mutual longing and desire as they read each other's thoughts during the wait for the cab: *I want you! What happens next? Where is this going?*

Minutes later, a horn sounded outside, and Grahame sprang up from the edge of the sofa.

'Right, that's us. Thanks again, Sharon. Catch you tomorrow I guess?'

'Yeah, I'm working from seven.'

He nodded.

Their time was up for tonight, and, in a matter of a few days, it would be up completely. Grahame and Mikey would be going back to Aberdeen ... and then? It would get complicated. But for now, he was still in town, and, as she stood on the doorstep waving off the cab till it was out of sight, Sharon already missed him with an ache.

'Ahh! I get it now! I thought you'd been quiet this past week. Course yer have! I might've known there was a bloke involved!' Trace cackled into her coffee at Sharon's kitchen table.

It was Friday lunchtime and, ever since Grahame had left last night, Sharon had thought of nothing but him. She'd tossed and turned without cease in the muggy heat, wishing he was next to her; her mind replaying that kiss over and over. 'It's not as simple as that,' she replied.

Trace pulled a face. 'Why? Is it a woman?'

Sharon pulled one back. 'No, it's not a bloody woman! What I mean is, he's not just any bloke. He's special.' She smiled as she pictured him, lovely Grahame. 'I've never felt a connection like this with anyone. I've really … fallen for him.'

Trace made a loud huffing sound. 'You fell for Mark Chandler a few backs an' all!'

Sharon shook her head, vehemently. 'That was purely physical, Trace. I told you; he was just an itch that needed scratching. This is different. We haven't even slept together and I …' She hesitated.

'What?'

She swallowed hard. Even *she* could not believe the enormity of what she was about to say. 'I think I'm falling in bloody love with him!'

Trace was speechless, her mouth agape. 'Well, don't tell *me*, tell him yer daft mare! You can't piss about with these things. When yer find happiness, you've gotta grab it by the balls.'

Sharon covered her beaming face with her hands and let out a muffled gasp. 'I'm going to! … Not grab him by the balls, I mean, as soon as

I see him tonight, I'm going to tell him exactly how I feel.' Her dreamy smile disintegrated as, just then, her phone started ringing on the kitchen countertop.

Trace's face lit up. 'Is that him? Is that Loverboy?'

'No, it won't be him. We haven't exchanged numbers, yet.'

She burst out laughing. 'You're in love with the fella and you don't even know his bloody phone number?! Oh God, that's good! That's a good one! I've heard it all, now.'

Sharon glanced at the caller ID. 'It's Mum. Hold that thought! … Hello?'

'Sharon! Sharon, love. You've gotta get over here quick! Right now. As soon as you can!' Sue's voice was frantic.

'Why?! What's the matter?!'

'It's your dad. It's his heart. We think it's his heart. I can't get any sense out of him.'

Sharon gulped. 'Have you called an ambulance?'

Trace's head shot up.

'Yes, it's on the way. Can you get over here, quick as you can? I'm frightened, love.'

'Hang on, Mum. I'm coming right now!'

Trace jumped up from her chair. 'Need a lift?'

'Please, yes. Let's go. Hurry!'

Trace pulled over into the layby outside Sharon's folks' place. 'I'll sit here with Izzy and wait till I hear from you.'

Sharon nodded, jumping out the car before it had even reached a complete stop. She flew up the garden path and in through the unlocked front door to the sitting room where Jim was now lying on his back on the sitting room floor.

'He's unconscious, Sharon!' Sue wailed, her eyes bulging in panic as she attempted something verging on CPR.

The ambulance still had not arrived.

Sharon pushed her aside and took over the CPR properly. Jim wasn't breathing and she couldn't feel a pulse, but she was shaking so much, she couldn't be sure if there was one or not. She gave mouth-to-mouth, before starting with chest compressions, recalling having once read somewhere that they should be performed at the same tempo as The Bee Gees' "Stayin' Alive". With it being a hot karaoke favourite at the Shangri-la, she could hear it bar for bar in her head.

'Is there a defibrillator close by?' Sharon called out to Sue.

Her face was blank. 'I don't know, love.'

'Okay, forget it.'

Sue rushed out of the room ... to be sick, Sharon assumed, but then she returned with the hoover ... the bloody hoover!

Sharon's mouth hung agape as she pumped. 'What the bloody hell you doing?!'

'Hoovering up for the paramedics,' she replied, brusquely, grappling to plug it in.

'How am I supposed to listen for breathing?!'

Sue nodded, tossed it into the kitchen and sparked up a fag. Sharon knew she'd be feeling powerless. She had to be doing something, *anything.*

'Come on, Dad. Fight!' Sharon yelled as she continued pounding his chest, alternating with mouth-to-mouth every thirty compressions. She watched closely for signs of life.

Nothing.

'They're coming!' Sue sighed, puffing frantically on her cigarette as sirens blared in the distance, drawing closer with every passing second.

Sharon kept on. Her arms ached and, already, she was exhausted, but she kept on; determined to save the life that had given her her own. Images of her childhood flashed in her mind with every compression: Jim teaching her to swim, to ride a bike, to be an ace at Scrabble.

'We'll take over from here, love.' The paramedics' voices brought her out from her head. She moved away, her shoulders slumping in relief, the rest of her rigid with fear.

Please, God. Please save him!

Sue looked more ashen than Jim. He was all she'd known. They'd fought like cat and dog, but they were like pen and paper: each pointless without the other.

As mother and daughter watched, heart-in-mouths, his lifeless body jolting with the shock of the defibrillator, the idea of being without him was unthinkable. Him not being sat in the armchair by the window watching Countdown, not watching the electric meter like a hawk, not rationing the bog roll, his sandy Crocs not lying in a heap at the back door. It was simply out of the question. He had to pull through and he would. Jim Taylor was made of strong stuff.

'We've only room for one in the ambulance,' said the female paramedic as the others juggled continuing CPR with getting Jim onto the stretcher.

'You go, Mum. I'll follow with Trace and Izzy.'

Sue nodded and Sharon hugged her tightly, watching through unspilled tears from the front doorstep as she hurriedly followed the stretcher down the garden path toward the ambulance.

Sharon put all her focus on just locking the front door and getting to hospital. She wouldn't cry. Not here. Not now. Not until there was something to cry about.

Trace was mostly silent during the drive to the hospital. She was a good time gal, a hurricane of fun. She didn't know how to act in a crisis. What was there to say that would make any difference? Nothing. Sometimes, there are no words.

As the car drew into the hospital car park, Sharon felt that familiar feeling. The last time she had arrived there, she'd had it: dread. Pure, unadulterated dread. Like Jim, she hated hospitals and she'd never imagined she would be back here so soon.

'Do you want me to stick around or would you rather I took Izzy back to mine?' Trace asked in a low voice.

'I've no idea how long we'll be here … the hospital's no place for kids. Best take her back to yours if that's okay?'

She nodded.

'Thank you.'

'Will Grandad Jim be okay?' Izzy asked from the back seat, her voice wobbling.

'Of course, he will,' Sharon replied, fraudulently confident. If she said it enough times, she would start to believe it: *he's going to be okay. He's going to be okay. He's going to be okay.*

'You want me to phone the camp for you?' Trace asked.

Oh, God. Shit! Work! 'Yes. Please, Trace.' She turned to face her friend, the lump in her throat expanding. 'I'll … be in touch.'

Trace gave a sombre nod as Sharon unfastened her belt and stepped out of the stuffy car into the cool evening air, hurrying toward the busy A&E department.

There was a queue. She couldn't stand still in it. Eventually she moved to the front. 'Hello. My Dad's just been admitted by ambulance. His names Jim. Jim Taylor.' Sharon could scarcely believe the words as they left her lips. 'My mum went with him in the ambulance. Do you know where they might be?'

'Take a seat. I'll see what I can find out for you.'

Sharon refused to sit. She stood instead. Standing made her feel as though she was doing more. She chewed her nails. She couldn't help it. She'd only just grown them enough to be worthy of gel polishes, but she was full of nervous energy, and it needed to be spent.

'Sharon Blewitt?' Came a small voice.

Ugh, that bloody name! 'Yes?'

'Your mother is asking for you. Please come this way.'

The petite, Filipino lady's eyes were kind and smiley beneath her face mask. It was obviously good news. *Thank God! They've stabilised him. It might be a two, maybe three-day stay, now. He wouldn't like that, but at least he'll be on the mend. He'll be back to his daily beach walks and moaning about inflation in no time.* She followed the woman around the corner and along a corridor, through a set of double doors, quickly losing her bearings after they'd walked for what felt like an age. Eventually, they arrived at a side room.

The Filipino lady opened the door and showed her inside, then left, closing it gently behind her with barely a click. Sharon took one look at Sue slumped in a chair in the corner and she knew. Something was gone from her eyes. She looked at Sharon and shook her head in confirmation rather than say the words out loud. He was gone.

Jim Taylor: the driest, wittiest, wisest, sarkiest, savviest personality on the planet had gone. And the world would never be the same again.

Lost at Sea

Chapter 15

The blurry image of her folks' spare bedroom came into view as Sharon opened her sleep-impoverished eyes. Izzy was still asleep in the twin single beside her. The room smelled just the same as it always had - clean linen infused with the slight mustiness of old fixtures and fittings and the residuum of Sue's chain-smoking. The sunlight streamed through the same gap in the curtains. The seagulls yattered. The milk float rattled. It was just another day. But he wasn't there: *Dad, Grandad Jim.* Wasn't in the house. Wasn't even in the world anymore. He'd been here one minute, larger than life, then gone the next. How could it be?

Sharon drifted downstairs to the kitchen for a glass of water and some painkillers for her pounding head. She'd spent the whole night crying because now, she had something to cry about.

Sue was hunched over the kitchen table with a cigarette. Her fourth, fifth, twentieth? Who knew.

The full cup of tea resting in front of her had grown a skin. 'Did you sleep?'

Sharon shook her head. 'You?'

'Not much. I kept waking up and remembering.'

She nodded.

'I just … don't know what to do with myself, love. I don't know what I should be doing. It's like the world's just stopped.'

Sharon lowered her gaze toward the back door where Jim's sandy Crocs still lay in a heap. They would never again contain his stubby, caveman feet. Never take him on another walk along the Golden Mile. He'd worn them every day for the past God-knows-how-long, but now they were redundant. Reality hit like a funfair dodgem. He would never walk through the back door again. The bangarang of his northern drawl would become but an echo. She could hear it now: *nothing lasts forever, kid.*

The ceaseless susurrations of the breaking waves, the hissing effervesces as they stretched out onto the wet sand before retreating back to repeat the cycle had a way of stilling the mind like nothing else could. Jim's was a great mind. It had needed a lot of stilling and this was the place he'd gotten it. Now more than ever, it was obvious why.

Sharon watched as Izzy picked up stones from the shore and threw them vigorously across the water till they broke the surface with loud *plonks*. Both father figures had gone from her life now. What was going on in that young mind of hers?

Sue wiped her swollen eyes with the back of her hand as she gazed out to sea. 'I don't know where he's gone to, Sharon, but if he were anywhere right now, he'd be here.'

A sudden breeze swept her hair back as though to confirm it; his spirit was here, in every ounce of water, in every grain of sand. 'I think we'll give him a low-key send off, love. You know your dad, he wouldn't want the fuss of a funeral … nor the expense, come to that.' Her chuckle was hollow. 'We'll have him cremated. Scatter his ashes at sea. It's what he would've wanted.'

Sharon nodded. 'Wild and free, just like the sea.'

Sue smiled sombrely and linked her daughter's arm, tightly. They only had each other now.

Hi Steve. Dad passed away last night. Apologies for the short notice but I'm going to need a few days to get my head together. I'll be be in touch. Thanks. Sharon.

It still didn't seem real, even as she read the text back. It was as though she was snooping through somebody else's messages. Not *her* dad. Not Jim Taylor. He was too much of a stubborn bugger to give up that easily. He was always going to live forever.

A reply pinged back in seconds:

Very sorry to hear that, Sharon. Take as long as you need.

The weekend passed in a hazy montage of halves: half-listened-to conversations, half-drunk cups of tea, half-eaten takeaways, half a night's sleep. And, as she woke late on Monday morning, still at her folks' and still with the same thick head she'd had ever since she'd taken that dreadful call, Sharon suddenly remembered: Grahame and Mikey were leaving today. Her head turned sharply toward the bedside clock: 10.05 AM. *Shit!* What would she do? Everything had changed. Now wasn't the time to be chasing men, but still, if she didn't catch him before he went, he'd be gone … just like everything else in her life. She needed to find him; even if only to explain what had happened.

In a panic, she flung back the bedcovers and pulled on yesterday's crumpled clothes which, given the feeling that nothing much mattered anymore, had been duly slung on the floor.

She gave her teeth the quickest brush of their life and bolted downstairs into the sitting room where Izzy was engrossed in her iPad, and Sue stared blankly at the television.

'I've got to pop out, Mum. There's something I've forgotten to do.' There was no time to wait for a response.

It was barely a two-minute drive to the train station. Sharon knew that they were leaving in the morning, but Grahame hadn't said what time.

She glanced at the clock on the dashboard: 10.21 AM. Maybe, just maybe they'd still be here!

She unclipped her belt and jumped out the car, then raced across the carpark into the station, scanning the area with desperate eyes.

No sign of them.

She dashed out onto the platform and surveyed the small crowd of waiting passengers.

Nothing.

Clutching her head in angst, her eyes travelled to the help desk. She dashed toward it. 'Excuse me, I was hoping to catch a friend here. I don't know what train he'd be taking; all I know is that he's heading for Aberdeen this morning. Do you know what train he might be on?'

The chap behind the booth sucked in his teeth. 'Blimey, Aberdeen you say? There ain't no single train from Yarmouth to Aberdeen, darlin'.'

Sharon didn't care for his patronising laugh and her look of disapproval wasn't wasted on him.

He gave a relenting sigh. 'He can only get a train to Norwich from here, love. Then I imagine it's gunna be Norwich to Peterborough from there, then Peterborough to Edinburgh, then Edinburgh to Aberdeen. It's a full day's travel. My guess is he'll be long gone.'

Her heart sank. 'Okay ... thanks.'

'Why don't you just give him a call, love?'

D 'oh ... piss off, Captain Obvious!

Gutted, Sharon turned and walked defeatedly back to the car. He was right. Grahame would be long gone. She'd missed the boat.

∞∞∞

By Wednesday, Sue seemed in a slightly better place. She threw herself into arranging Jim's send-off and had even organised for a bench to be erected in his favourite spot along the promenade in his memory.

By comparison, though she'd felt able to return to her own place and to go back to work, Sharon was lost. She was learning first-hand that you don't know what you've got till it's gone. How happy she'd been prior to that dreadful call on Friday lunchtime, and she hadn't been her own boss at the time; she'd had a part-time bar job. And there was no big house by the sea; the social paid the rent on her two-bed terrace because she couldn't. There had been no top-of-the-range SUV parked out front; she didn't even own a car. But none of that had even crossed her mind. Jim was still in the world. Grahame was still in town. All she wanted, more than anything else in the world, was for them both to still be here.

'When are you going to have someone come and clean me bastard windows?!'

Nothing ever changes here, Sharon thought to herself as she weaved through the angry crowd of guests at reception on what was her first shift since Jim's passing.

'I'm afraid we don't have any cleaners on site. They clock off at three,' the receptionist countered.

'Clock off at three? There's enough work ter keep 'em 'ere till next bloody year!'

'Well, if you come back tomorrow morning…'

'Come back? You want *me* to come back? I'm on me 'olidays, darlin'! D'ya know what? Sod it! Keep the beggars dirty. At least then we won't have ter look out at this shithole.'

Though she felt like turning around and walking straight back out, Sharon gritted her teeth and made her way through to the bar. She didn't know what the Shangri-la's policy for sick pay was, but if it was like everything else around here, it would be a joke. Best to keep busy. Keep earning.

Darren from the ents team was first to offer his condolences. Then Kelly. Then Jeanette … Sharon was surprised the old boot had it in her, but grateful, nonetheless.

Within five minutes, it felt like she'd never left. The same old cheesy holiday park favourites blasted from the PA system to which the ents team busted the same crap moves. There were the same old complaints of flat beer, too much head on pints and lipstick on glasses, but *he* wasn't here, lovely Grahame with his pint of Carling. Sharon stared longingly at the bar stool he'd sat on while they talked away her shift that time. The old git who was sat in it currently looked up and smiled invitingly, thinking his luck was in.

Good, God!

He winked. 'Another one in 'ere when yer ready, duck.'

She took his glass and pulled him a fresh pint of Guinness. 'Four fifty, please.'

He made a performance of making his card payment. 'Sorry, duck. Doesn't seem ter wanna work, I'm not ignorin' yer.'

She wished he was!

'I'll try givin' it a rub. When yer rub it, the magic 'appens.' He paired his throaty chuckle with another seedy wink and Sharon was almost sick in her mouth.

'Ah, Sharon. Good to have you back,' came Steve the bar manager's voice from behind.

Of course, it was. It meant that, once again, he had the best job in the world!

'Hiya, Steve.'

'How you bearing up?'

'Fine, thanks.'

They both knew she wasn't, but she could hardly respond to tell him *shit, Steve. Really fucking shit, actually.*

He looked thoughtful for a moment as he placed both hands inside his trouser pockets and began to rummage, and for one dreadful moment, Sharon began to worry that he had advanced to pleasuring himself in public … until he pulled out what appeared to be a small, folded piece of paper.

'Listen, before I forget, a Scottish chap came to the bar asking after you. I didn't tell him about your dad because … well, that sort of thing's private, isn't it? Anyway, he gave me this to pass on to you.' He flourished the paper toward her.

In normal circumstances, Sharon wouldn't dream of touching anything that had come from Steve's trouser pockets, but, given that it was from Grahame, lovely Grahame, she couldn't grab it quick enough. Matter of fact, she was so chuffed, she could've kissed Steve's shiny, bald nut!

'Did he say anything else?'

'No, that was it.'

'Okay, cheers. Ta.'

Sharon waited until he'd gone before she unfolded the note. It was a phone number written in handwriting as neat as he was. Grahame had wanted her to have his phone number … which meant he wanted to hear from her! And he would, just as soon as it was an appropriate time to call.

Next morning, among the usual crop of bills and circulars, came an important-looking letter. Sharon stared down at the logo printed on the envelope and wasted no time opening it. A few sentences in, she wished he hadn't bothered. It was from Stella's solicitor. She was seeking to exercise her visitation rights to Izzy as her grandparent. What the hell?! Stella couldn't give a monkey's about Izzy! Never did ... at least not beyond medicating her for invented illnesses, anyway. They'd never been close. Never had what you could call a relationship. This wasn't about spending time with her grandchild, Sharon knew exactly what Stella's game was: she wanted to poison Izzy's mind. Turn her against her mum. Drive a wedge between them, just as she believed Sharon had done between her and Gary. It was her fault Gary was in prison. She'd driven him to it. And this would be the perfect revenge: an eye for an eye. Well, not if Sharon had any say in it! Over her dead body would Stella have access to Izzy. If Izzy wanted to see the horrible old cow when she turned eighteen, it would be her choice to make. But for now, no chance!

Sharon was seething. And, as the first of the day's unchanging strains of Rick Astley resonated through the walls, she became incensed with anger. 'Who does she think she is?! How bloody dare she!' She crashed around the house as she gathered up the dirty laundry to put a wash on.

'She's got some brass neck!' She fumed, stomping down the stairs with her arms full of clothes and her mind full of rage. She filled the drum of the washing machine, chucked in a laundry capsule and set it off to wash. It was a good ten minutes later before she realised that she'd put her work trousers in to wash … with Grahame's number still in the damn pocket.

Oh, fuck! Fuuuuuuck!

She flew through to the kitchen, letting out a pained howl as she watched the drum turning the saturated, soapy laundry inside. In a panic, she lurched forward and switched off the machine at the plug. The drum stopped moving but the half-drum of water remained. Of course, it would. It wasn't going anywhere until the cycle had finished.

'Aghhhhhh!' She threw her hands up to her face, buried her head in them and slumped to the floor. Then, an idea came to her...

'Shangri-la, Chloe speaking,' came the lethargic voice at the end of the line.

'Yeah, hi. I wonder if you can help. One of your guests gave me their telephone number to call them about something and I … *washed it* … er, lost it. I was wondering if there was any chance you could look them up on your system and give me the telephone number, please?' Sharon's voice was polite and hopeful.

'No, sorry. We can't give out guests' details. It's against GDPR regulations.'

'Pardon?' *Since when did the Shangri-la give a shit about regulations?!*

'We can't give out that sort of information.'

'But ... but I work there. I work behind the bar,' Sharon tried.

'Doesn't make any odds. We're still not allowed to share guests' personal data.'

Grrr ... as if they weren't in the business of selling it on anyway!

'Right. Thanks.' Sharon slammed down the phone and sighed deeply. 'Thanks for bloody nothing!'

There had to be some other way to contact Grahame. Sharon already knew that he wouldn't be on social media. He'd said in conversation more than once that he wasn't into all that. But it didn't stop her trying. She searched for him on every social media platform she knew of, and when that yielded nothing, she Googled him. Then she looked on LinkedIn. There were plenty of Grahame Murrays, but none of them him; none of them lovely Grahame. She knew he worked in engineering but there was no end of engineering firms in Aberdeen, and he'd never mentioned which it was. She could hardly ring round all of them on the off chance that a Grahame Murray who looks a bit like Colin Farrell works there, and, if he does, could they please have him call her back because she needs to tell him that she thinks she might be in love with him ... Christ, no.

She chewed her lip and thought about it. There

was one thing left to try.

∞ ∞ ∞

"Ello, Blondie. What can I do yer for?' Mark Chandler smiled, looking up from his desk in surprise.

Sharon gently closed the office door behind her. 'I need a favour, Mark. A *big* favour.'

He relaxed back into his office chair and stared at her quizzically under sexy, furrowed brows – though they weren't half as sexy as they used to be, Sharon had decided. She'd gone right off him.

He flashed his smile; not half as winning as it had once been, either. 'A big favour, eh? I gave you one of those not so long ago, didn't I?'

She let out her breath impatiently while he laughed at the bad joke. 'I need a telephone number. A guest's telephone number. I asked reception but they wouldn't give it out. Said it was against GDPR regulations or something.'

He nodded, seemingly impressed. 'Good to hear they're doing their jobs properly … for once.'

She stared at him for a few moments. 'Listen, Mark. It's not a big deal. I had the number originally, but I lost it. It's not like it'd be unsolicited, they're expecting my call.'

'Who?'

She hesitated. 'It doesn't matter.'

Mark laughed. 'Doesn't look that way to me!'

She rolled her eyes. She might've known he would be difficult.

His chair squeaked as he sat forward in it. 'What's the name, then?' He picked up a pen and poised it over the sticky note pad on his desk.

Her face lit up. 'It's Grahame. Grahame Murray.'

His perma-smirk seemed to disintegrate off his face. 'It's a bloke?'

'Yeah … and?'

He let his pen fall out of his hands in apparent disgust. 'What sort of operation d'ya think I'm running here?'

Sharon looked at him in dismay, anger suddenly flaring in her chest. 'Oh, I know exactly what sort of operation you're running, Mark Chandler! But I don't say anything. Nobody does. Maybe they ought to.'

He tutted. 'Sounds like you're blackmailing me, Blondie.'

'I know what you get up to Mark, and I keep my mouth shut about it … just saying.'

He stared at her briefly. 'Look, I've got Mick Hendry on my back enough as it is. Fat old bastard's looking for an excuse to sack me and, right now, he ain't got one good enough. I need it to stay that way, Sharon. If he gets wind that I'm doling out guest information and risking landing the business with a pissing great fine, I'll be out on me arse.'

Sharon let out a deep sigh. Mark had been her

last chance. If he didn't get her the number, it was game over.

Suddenly, the perma-smirk was back. 'What's it worth?'

'Sorry?'

He looked down into his lap and brazenly unzipped his trousers.

Sharon stared at him, mouth agape. He was joking, surely?

He glanced at his flashy watch and nodded toward his lap. 'Well, go on, then. It ain't gonna pleasure itself … much as I'd love it to.'

She shook her head incredulously and turned on her heel. 'You're disgusting!' She could hear him still laughing from the other side of the door after she'd slammed it on her way out.

Suddenly, she felt filthy for having let a rotten, misogynistic pig like Mark Chandler anywhere near her. How didn't she see it? How could she have been so bloody stupid?! First Gary, then him. How was Sharon Taylor such a magnet for arseholes?!

Grahame had been the first and only real gentleman she'd come across. But, when he didn't hear from her, he would assume that she wasn't interested. Short of hiking to the Scottish Highlands with a wanted person poster, there was nothing she could do. It could have all been so perfect, but alas, it wasn't to be.

∞∞∞∞

Sue patted down her hair in the hallway mirror and wiped away a tear.

'Come on mum, let's go and get it done. He'll be itching to get down to the beach again,' Sharon prompted from the front doorstep.

Nodding, she brought out the urn from under her arm and clutched it tightly as she moped out of the door.

Sharon locked it and she, Sue and Izzy made their way to the Quay where a boat was waiting to take them out to sea.

'Lovely day for it, ain't it?' The skipper grinned.

Sue glared at him. No day's a lovely day when you're scattering your husband's ashes, but bless him, he was only trying to be nice. He had a jolly, rosy face and, with his white-grey beard, he reminded Sharon of Captain Birds Eye.

The boat chugged out of the quay and, before too long, they were out on the open sea.

Sue had put her hair in curlers the night before especially, but the strong breeze had already blown her honey-blonde waves to nothing.

When the boat was in position adjacent to the golden mile, the captain stopped the engine and the boat slowed, bobbing and rocking on the waves. Izzy took out the poem she had written and looked up at Sue who gave her granddaughter an encouraging nod. She cleared her throat and began to read…

> *'When you look for me and I am not there*
> *Do not grieve, do not despair*
> *Take a walk on the beach, dip your toes in the sand*
> *And you will feel me close at hand,*
> *When you call my name and there's no reply*
> *Hear the waves and do not cry*
> *For I am not lost, I didn't leave*
> *Now and forever, I am part of the sea.'*

A tearful round of applause followed Izzy's poignant words and Sue held out the urn over the water in readiness. 'There you are, Jim. Let the sea set you free.' She closed her eyes, drew in a deep breath, and tipped the ashes out over the side of the boat … only for the wind to blow a large quantity of them back inside onto everyone on board. They all stood wafting the air frantically and Sharon recoiled in horror as she observed Captain Bird's Eye who was now wearing Jim's ashes in his bloody great beard!

'D'ya know, I've spent many a year clearing up after your dad, but I never thought I'd sweep him up in a dustpan and brush,' Sue reflected over a Gin and tonic in Pub on The Prom afterwards.

Sharon looked at her and the two of them fell into fits of bittersweet giggles. 'I know I shouldn't … but all I can see is that skipper picking bits out of his beard for days to come.'

Sometimes, laughter is the best medicine.

Land Ahoy

Chapter 16

The trouble with havin' a taste of summink good, is that a taste is never enough: you're always left wanting the lot! Though Trace's motto had been meant it in a food sense, it was certainly ringing true for Sharon in a Grahame sense. It had been weeks since he'd left, but her mind's eye remembered his smile. Her skin remembered his touch and her lips remembered his kiss. She couldn't unfeel him. Couldn't just turn him off like a switch, even if she'd wanted to. And no matter how she busied herself, he was never far from her thoughts.

'Jim Beam please, darlin'. Make it a triple,' said the chap at the bar. Though he was dressed smartly, he was rough around the edges – a bit like a Bond villain, Sharon decided. She glanced down at his Rolex and then at his sovereign rings and wondered why he looked so pissed off for someone who clearly did alright for himself. And why was he drinking triple shots at 11:58 AM? Whoever he was, she could tell he'd been a bit of a hard man in his prime and she noticed that staff members had been acting strangely ever since he showed up: walking into the clubhouse, then making a swift U-turn.

'You're new here, aren't you?' He said, in a deep, gruff voice that meant business.

'I am, yes.'

'Thought so. You don't look useless enough to work here.'

Sharon laughed. 'Cheers.'

The man reached his hand across the bar. 'Mick Hendry ... and you are?'

Ah. Now she understood.

'I'm Sharon. Sharon Blew...' she managed to stop herself before she fully said it. 'Sharon Taylor.'

Mick nodded, shaking her hand. 'So, how'd they manage to get a pretty face like you working here, then?'

She felt her cheeks colour. 'Well, my life's pretty much gone down the pan this year. I had to get a job to support me and my daughter and this was all I could get.'

Mick threw his head back and laughed. Sharon often came across as blunt when she was nervous, which he'd mistaken for balls and honesty. Mick Hendry loved balls ... but only the courage kind. 'Your life fell apart, did it? Well, I've gotta say, I'm intrigued.' He looked across the bar at her, quizzically.

Sharon chewed her lip. The whole town knew her business. What was one more person? 'Well, my husband of twenty years has just gone down for fraud.'

'Oh?'

'Yeah, he'd basically been living a double life. Romancing wealthy widows. Conned them out of hundreds of thousands of pounds.'

It seemed to evoke some sort of recollection in Mick. 'Ah, yes. The geezer with the B&B. The er …' he trailed off, then clicked his fingers, 'Driftwood, right?'

Chuff me. The guys an expat and even he bloody knows! 'That's right, yeah.'

He gave a contemplative whistle. 'Greed. Makes people do crazy things.'

Sharon sighed, reflectively. 'I loved that place. It was my baby. Put my heart and soul into it.'

'You was doing alright an' all, wasn't yer? I saw the piece in the Mercury online.'

Sharon looked surprised. 'You did?'

'Oh, yes! I always like to keep abreast of what's going on in the town while I'm away.'

Oh good. At least the scandal hasn't reached Europe!

'Well, it was going really well. We were rated five on Tripadvisor, you know.' Sharon had lost count of the number of times she'd told people that. It was her little triumph.

Mick's eyes widened. 'Really? Cor, blimey. You must've been doing something right. What's the secret?'

'An outstanding customer experience.' She was unhesitating.

He nodded. Now he could see that she was more than just a pretty face.

'Well, it's like I was always saying to my husband, *forget cutting corners, forget profit. We've got to speculate to accumulate. Put the customer at the heart of everything we do. They're our business. Without them, we've got nothing.* You've got to go out of your way. Think outside the box. Don't just take their money and run, give them an amazing experience they'll never forget in exchange for their business. Because, you know what? We're in an age where people love to document their lives. Love to share their experiences. So, if you've given them a bad one, you'd better run for the hills 'cos the whole world's gonna get to know about it. But if it's outstanding, then it's the best form of free advertising you'll ever get and, boom! The profit's taken care of itself.' She paused for breath. 'Why would you not strive to be outstanding every time?'

Mick placed his whiskey glass down on the bar and applauded her with his massive hands. This bird might've been petite, but he could see that she was whip-smart and savvy. Just the sort of person he needed on board his sinking ship.

'Tell you what, Sharon,' he said, folding his chunky arms which were deeply tanned and freckled from years of the Spanish sun. 'I might have a business proposition for you … if you're game, that is.'

'A business proposition?' She parroted back at him. 'What sort of a business proposition?'

'Well, it's like this, Sharon. I'm a man on a mission. I've flown in from Marbella to grab this place by the bollocks, if you'll pardon my French. Sort it out once and for all. Get shot of the deadwood and bring in business-minded people like yourself. Turn the place around. Know what I mean?'

She nodded, enthusiastically.

He looked around the clubhouse behind him. 'I'm ashamed to say that I've all but given up on this place. I've sat and watched it go to rack and ruin over the years. It was a case of out of sight, out of mind, you know? But the thing is, I don't like to lose, Sharon. I like to win. I want to be the best.'

She knew the feeling.

'I want my park to be the biggest and best for miles around and I reckon you can help me out with that.'

Sharon pressed her index finger to her clavicle. 'Me? You want *me* to help you?'

'You, bet your boots I do.'

'Why me?'

He chuckled. 'Well, they do say that behind every man is a strong woman, Sharon, but I'd say these days it's the other way around, wouldn't you? If you can do with my park what you did with that B&B of yours, I'll make you managing director. I've got the capital; you've clearly got the business acumen. If we make a success of it, who knows? We could be opening parks up and down the country. I believe it! I can see it now, Sharon. Whaddya say? Do you think you could do something with this place?' His voice was elevated, excited. He certainly seemed to have a lot of faith in her to say that they'd literally known each other five minutes. But was it faith or desperation? Sharon guessed it was the latter. She swallowed hard. Mick Hendry didn't look like the sort of bloke you want to be on the wrong side of. What if it didn't work out? Still, this place was at rock bottom. She couldn't make it any worse. 'But what about Mark?'

'Clearing out his office as we speak. I've just sacked him.'

'Jeez!'

Mick took a gulp of his whisky and gasped as it burned all the way down his throat. 'I'd been looking for an excuse to give him his cards for a while now. Last thing this place needs is a playboy like him running the show. Anyway, Brenda found a bag of Charlie in his desk drawer last week, and it was *nos vemos, Don Juan!* It's like I said, Sharon, I'm getting shot of the deadwood. This place needs a workforce with drive and ambition, not a bunch of bloody numpties.' He tapped his nose with a giant finger. 'I know what's what. Let's just say, I have me moles.'

It wasn't hard to guess who the mole was. Why

else would he employ a woman in her sixties with a fondness for standing around gossiping to lead the cleaning team?'

'So, whaddya say, Sharon? You up for the challenge?'

She smiled knowingly; there was nothing to lose and perhaps, something priceless to be gained.

The holiday season had drawn to a close. Trade wound down for winter whilst the town caught its breath. But Sharon Taylor wasn't winding down. No, siree! She was only just getting started.

As she rolled through the entrance gate of what was soon to be the all-new Sand Scapes Holiday Park in the polar white Mercedes-AMG C 63 coupe that Mick Hendry had financed as her company car, there was something right at the top of a very long list of things on her agenda.

She drew up at reception and stepped out of the car in a grey power suit, smiling pleasantly at all the builders and workmen who were busy getting the transformation underway. She too was undergoing a transformation. She was getting her independence back and it was a good feeling being able to provide for herself and Izzy.

Mick Hendry had put her in touch with his

pukka brief and she hadn't heard a thing from Stella's solicitor ever since. All was as well as it could've been, but there was still something she needed to do.

She grabbed herself a coffee from the machine in reception and, as she stood looking out of her office window across the leaden November sky, she smiled to herself, because there, tightly ensconced in the palm of her right hand, lay a yellow post-it note with Grahame Murray's telephone number written on it.

When she'd accepted Mick Hendry's business proposition, Sharon hadn't done it for the money. Nor for the Mercedes C 63 coupe. The principal thing at the forefront of her mind when she'd said *yes* had been the thought of getting Grahame's telephone number. He was all she wanted in the world right now.

As she sipped her coffee, she wondered what he was doing right now. Did he still think about her? Ten weeks had passed since they'd last seen or spoke to one another, would he even want to hear from her now? Would he believe the mountainous task she'd had just getting his number to call him? There was only one way to find out.

Her hands shook as she tapped the numbers listed on the paper into the keypad of her phone. She drew in a deep breath and exhaled deeply to calm her rising nerves. *Right, here we go!* She braced herself to hear his voice again, but her face fell as the call went straight to voicemail. She had no idea how she was going to word this and, as the beep followed, it all came tumbling out in a torrent of stutters. 'Um, yeah, Grahame, hi. It's Sharon. Sharon from Yarmouth? I, um. You're not going to believe this, but I've been trying to reach you ever since you and Mikey left. I looked for you at the train station on the Monday but … Dad … my D-dad died. He had a heart attack on the Friday night. That's why I didn't come in to work for a few days. I couldn't … I … had to get my head together. But then I came back, and Steve gave me your number but I,' she sighed incredulously. 'I put it in the washing machine with my work trousers and it's taken me all this time to get your number again. Anyway, I just wanted you to know that … I just … I think I'm in love with you Grahame. I'll understand if you don't feel the same but just … just give me a call when you get this, will you? Thanks.'

As she ended the call, Sharon had a horrible thought: what if Grahame had a new number? People swap networks all the time. What if she'd just poured her heart out to some unknown person who'd acquired Grahame's old number? Hm. No, realistically, the chances were it was still Grahame's number. He'd get the message and he'd call back. The call would come soon, any time soon.

But it didn't.

Days passed and, though her phone was always on her, and she checked it constantly, Sharon didn't hear back from Grahame. But why? She couldn't understand it. Did he think she was messing him around? Had she dented his ego? She tortured herself with the same questions: *What if this? What if that?* But it looked as though she'd never know.

∞∞∞∞

'Barry's takin' me ter Turkey!' Trace announced over a mouthful of Chicken Chow Mein. It was Friday night and Sharon had not long finished work. Izzy was staying with Sue and, rather than spend the evening alone, Sharon called in company and a Chinese takeaway. She smiled. She was pleased for Trace, despite the shortcomings in her own life where romance was concerned. 'Great. When are you going?'

'Couple of weeks' time.'

Sharon nodded. 'For how long?'

Trace seemed to hesitate a touch before she said it. 'A month.'

'Wow.'

'Well, Barry ain't seen his family in ages, so it's time with them as much as it is a getaway for the two of us.'

Sharon looked at her friend over the rim of her wine glass and suddenly lost her appetite. *A month. What am I going to do without her for a whole month?!*

She knew what her dad would tell her: *we come into this world alone and we leave alone. Get used to your own company, kid.* She wished she'd inherited just an ounce of his hardiness.

Trace quickly changed the subject. 'How's it going at the Shangri-la, then?'

'Busy,' Sharon replied, her shoulders slumping exaggeratedly. 'The site's the same but it'll be a whole new park. It's got a new name, new branding, new theming. I've got so many ideas, Trace. I don't even know if we'll have everything finished by March.'

She chuckled. 'You ain't gonna bankrupt that Hendry fella before you've even opened, are yer?'

Sharon threw her a jocose look of dread. 'Yeah, can you imagine? He'd be swapping Marbella for Margate!' She chuckled. 'Nah. Mick personally approves everything before it gets the go-ahead. He knows it's a big investment.'

Trace wrinkled her nose. 'I dunno why he didn't just sell that dump and enjoy his cash. That's what I'd have done. I mean, he obviously don't need the money.'

Sharon smiled, pensively. Throughout the town, Mick Hendry was known as *That Pillock with the Shangri-la*, and she was known as *The Fraudster's Wife*. Neither was in it for the money. They wanted victory … it was far sweeter.

Sharon stood under the shelter of the doorstep as

Trace tottered out to her cab. The rain was coming down in sheets and the wind was blowing a gale. She gave her friend a final wave as she dived into the car for cover, quickly slamming the door behind her.

With a rattle of the exhaust, the cab pulled away and, shivering from the blast of cold, Sharon closed and locked the front door. As she busied herself clearing away the wine bottles and remnants of the Chinese takeaway, the doorbell rang. She quickly unloaded the contents of her arms onto the kitchen worktop and hurried back to the front door.

'What you forgot...' her voice trailed off and she froze in surprise as she came face to face with Grahame. His dark hair was plastered to his face and his leather jacket wet from the rain. Without hesitation, she pulled him inside by his shirt. The door slammed behind him and neither said a word as they lunged toward one another. There was no time for conversation, too much had been wasted already. He grabbed her face with his cold hands, and they devoured each other like there was no tomorrow. Grahame was kind but this kiss was cruel, hungry, urgent; *vicious* even. His jacket fell heavily to the floor, and they kissed their way upstairs in a concert of popping buttons, neither of them willing to let go of the other; it had been too long. They fell onto the bed in a breathless tangle of limbs, embroiled in a storm of passion, deaf to the rain lashing against the windows;

unhearing of the howling wind that made the mature house out-moan them.

Sharon had lain awake in the small hours of many a sleepless night picturing this moment, but the reality unfolding between the sheets far outshone the fantasy. After all, how could she picture what she'd never had? Having sex with Gary Blewitt had been like shagging Winne the Pooh!

Grahame didn't just kiss her lips; he kissed her soul. He didn't just touch; he nurtured. He seemed to know his way around her body as if they'd always been lovers. And, as waves of pleasure crashed over her, she realised she had joined Trace's *Screamer's Club* without even trying!

Sharon had often heard it said that there's a world of contrast between having sex and making love and finally, she knew the difference. 'Can I take it you got my voicemail?' She laughed, lying encased in his arms after. The storm raged on outside, but she was safe as houses.

'Aye. I couldnay believe it. I'd all but given up on ye.'

She stroked his arm, reflectively. 'I didn't think you were going to call back.'

'I'm no so good on the phone, hen. I prefer tae huv conversations face tae face, ye know?'

There hadn't been much of that so far … but plenty of body talk!

Sharon gave a pensive sigh, her head rising in synchrony with his breathing as she lay on his chest. 'So, what happens now?'

'Er … we go tae sleep? … Unless ye need a stiff drink after that?'

She laughed. 'I mean with us. Do long-distance relationships ever work?'

He leaned down and kissed her forehead. 'Doesnay matter where you are darlin', I'm yours.'

Long Time no Sea

Chapter 17

Mick Hendry stood beside the marble water fountain at the entrance to the all-new Sand Scapes Holiday Park and allowed himself a smile. Victory was not yet his, but with its arresting signage and huge welcome sign against a backdrop of rock walls, contemporary uniformed gardens and solar lighting, his new park looked the dog's bollocks. It had been a big job and Mick's sentiments that it was one best overseen by a woman had clearly been spot on.

The new holiday park had set tongues wagging, but it was Mick Hendry's association with *The Fraudster's Wife* that had been talk of the town. What was he thinking of going into business with *her*? Stupid bugger must've finally lost his mind.

They'd soon see. They all would.

Mick popped open a bottle of Moet & Chandon in the new bar while a photographer from the local press snapped away and a journalist stood taking notes. 'You could hear a pin drop in here now, but just you wait! This place is gunna be rocking in peak season. We've got some headliners performing this year.'

'Oh really? Can you share?' The journalist's pen was poised over his notepad.

Mick sucked his teeth in. 'Well, we've got Peter Andre…' he paused, motioning toward the journalist's pen which hadn't yet budged. 'Well, go on then, stick it down on yer jotter, son.'

The journalist shook his head. 'If we could just stick to the headliners Mr Hendry so we stay within the word limit for the article.'

'Whaddya mean? He *is* a bleedin' headliner, son. You wanna see how much he's setting me back!' Mick flicked his head toward Sharon. 'Anyway, he weren't my first choice, it was this numpty, here. I reckon she wants ter be his mysterious girl.'

Not half! Well, fifteen years ago, at least. Sharon's bedroom walls had been covered in his posters.

The journalist raised a brow and started scribbling.

'That's it, keep writing, son. We've got Fleur East, Jason Donovan,' Mick continued. 'We've got comedians, Strictly stars, Britain's Got Talent finalists … oh, and we've managed ter get Rick Astley an' all … now he *was* me first choice. The ladies are gunna go potty for him.'

Sharon rolled her eyes. She had already gone potty from hearing the git every day for the last eight months. Still, at least he'd only perform the song once.

Aside from Sharon, Brenda was the only other member of staff at the Shangri-la to make it onto Sand Scapes' payroll because, in Micks own words, he hadn't *spent a shit-loada dough just ter have that bunch er numbskulls fuck everything up again*. And he knew that if any new staff member put a foot out of line, Brenda would ensure he was first to know about it. Sharon watched as she led the new cleaning team through the clubhouse.

It was a clean slate. New fixtures, new fittings, new faces; new everything. Finally, Sand Scapes was ready to rock 'n' roll and Sharon was looking forward to welcoming the first guests on opening day the next afternoon ... two very special guests in particular.

The reception staff looked soigné in their pristine yellow and blue co-ordinates. Every guest was greeted with a handshake and made to feel like they were VIPs regardless of which grade of accommodation they had booked. The relaxing background music with gentle ocean sounds created an essence of calm that was a globe away from the carnage it had once been. There were colour co-ordinated easy chairs, bean bags, water dispensers and complimentary bowls of sweets in the waiting area, and the six-hundred-gallon custom saltwater fish tank installed in the rear wall of reception wasn't wasted on kids and grown-ups alike. The entire guest experience had been carefully constructed so that the message was loud and clear from the outset: *you matter, and we care.*

Sharon had not seen Grahame since Valentine's Day weekend. They'd spent Christmas together as a four with Izzy and Mikey and, beyond that, snatched one weekend together a month. It wasn't enough. She wanted to kiss him goodnight in person each night, not through Facetime. She wanted to wake up next to him every morning and for him be the first person she saw. She craved him. Pined for him. Wanted all of him. They'd known from the get-go that it would be complicated and, for now, this was as good as it got. Some of Grahame was better than none of him, and when he and Mikey arrived at reception later that afternoon for a week-long break, they were shown to their accommodation personally by the managing director.

'I've given you a cheeky upgrade!' She grinned as they arrived outside the log cabin. 'You'll be pleased to know it's got a Playstation, Mikey.'

'Whoa, awesommme!'

She threw Grahame a kittenish look. 'And a hot tub.'

He met the look with an inviting smile. 'This

place is fantastic. You've done grand, babe. I'm proud of ye.'

She wrapped her arms around him and squeezed him tight, burying her face into his chest and breathing him in. 'I've missed you so much.'

∞ ∞ ∞

That evening, as they reclined beneath the stars in the hot tub, the silence was unusually tense.

'I need you, Sharon. Move in with me and Mikey. You and Izzy. Come tae Aberdeen,' Grahame blurted.

She let out a deep sigh. 'I can't Grahame. You know I can't. My life's here ... Mum needs me.'

He nodded. 'I know. And you've been there for yer ma since yer da passed, but ye cannay be there forever. What about your own happiness? We're sorted in Aberdeen. I've a good job, ma mortgage is nearly paid up. Ye wouldnay huv tae work. You and Izzy could slip in easy.'

Sharon gave a slight gasp. 'I love you Grahame and I need you too, but I don't want to just slip into your life. I don't want to be kept. I want to work ... I've always worked. I like my independence.'

'Fine. Ye can get a job in Aberdeen. Ye can get a job anywhere.'

He's right but ... 'I can't leave Mum, Grahame. She's lost her husband. She can't lose her daughter and grandchild as well.'

He said nothing and the silence returned, leaving only the sound of the bubbles whirring beneath them and the distant strains of music resonating from the clubhouse.

'This was always going to be complicated,' Sharon mumbled.

'I know,' he agreed, glumly. 'But when ye love someone ...'

She turned her head to face him. 'When you love someone, what? Are you saying that I should be the one to give everything up for you?' Her voice was calm but irked. This was the stubborn side of her which Jim had blessed her with.

Grahame held up his hands, defensively. 'No. No, that's no what I'm saying at all.'

'So, what, then?'

'Look, Sharon. I've got a loada ties up home. There's ma job. Mikey's settled at school. And Tilly ... Tilly's grave's up there. I cannay just up sticks. It's no as simple as that.'

Sharon drained the last of her glass of Prosecco. She understood, but she had always known that it would come to this. 'Well, then,' she sighed, pulling herself to her feet and climbing out of the hot tub, 'I can't see how this is going to work out.' She wrapped a towel around her shivering body and padded along the decking, back to the log cabin so that he wouldn't see her cry.

Grahame let out a long sigh and necked the rest of his glass in one gulp. He didn't have the answer.

∞ ∞ ∞

We need to talk x

The text woke Sharon from a restless night's sleep. She'd hated spending the night away from Grahame when he was here in town. It was such a waste when every moment together was so precious. But it was delayed self-preservation. She feared ending up hurt again and she was angry at herself. She'd done it again, hadn't she? Dived in headfirst without knowing the depth of the water. Now she could see that it was too shallow. The long distance only allowed them to be half-in, half-out. Never fully immersed; and it could never be that way unless something changed. But there was no easy solution. She couldn't expect Grahame to uproot himself and Mikey. Could they keep going as they were? How long would it be before the relationship ran out of steam? Part-time love worked for some people, but it was never going to be enough for Sharon, and it wasn't fair on either of them, or the kids, to carry on something that couldn't last. Maybe it was better to just end it here. Sharon could feel the walls creeping up again. Grahame felt like 'the one.' There was no doubt in her mind. But there was no way to move forward beyond this limbo.

Okay. Let's talk. Where and when? x

Can you and Izzy meet us at the Pleasure Beach at 1pm? x

It was a strange arrangement for hosting relationship crisis talks, but hm, okaaay.

'Listen, I dinnay want us tae fight, Sharon and I promise we'll find a solution tae this, okay?' Grahame's voice was sincere. He looked her in the eye as he pulled down the safety bar.

She nodded and hoped he was right.

As the rollercoaster began its clunky ascent up the first climb, Sharon gazed sombrely out to sea. She thought of Jim and smiled. Was he watching over her? As they climbed higher still, she screwed her eyes tightly shut.

Grahame gave a weary tut. 'Whit did I tell ye about keepin yer eyes closed?'

Sharon frowned. 'What?'

'Ye miss all the fun!'

She opened them and turned to face him, noticing that he was smiling strangely. He nodded toward the open red velvet jewellery box which he was clasping tightly in his hands and Sharon let out a surprised gasp as she saw the engagement ring twinkling in the spring sunshine.

'Marry me?'

There was no time to reply as the rollercoaster plunged down the first hill. Sharon caught her breath as it levelled out again. 'But … but …'

'I'll put the hoose on the market, Sharon. There's plenty engineering firms in Yarmouth. And I've hud a long talk wi Mikey, he's given his blessing and he's happy tae make the move doon here.' Grahame had to shout to be heard over the noise of the ride.

'And Tilly?'

'She's no really there, is she?' He looked up at the sky with a sanguine smile. 'She's everywhere.'

Sharon blinked back at him, lost for words.

'Well? Is it a yes, or no? Quick! Before the Headchopper!' Grahame stuffed the ring box back into his jacket pocket as the train gathered up speed again.

Sharon beamed. Her eyes watering from both the ride and happy tears. 'Course it's a bloody yeeeeeeeeeeees!' The coaster plummeted down the hill, taking the last of her breath away. As it flew around the rest of the track, she looked out to sea once more. The vast body of water seemed to twinkle in a way it hadn't before: Jim approved!

When the coaster arrived back at the station, Grahame jumped out of the car onto the platform and got down on one knee. 'I couldnay do this on the ride,' he explained, 'bit tricky! But you're still getting the full experience.'

Sharon laughed, watching as he fumbled in his pocket and took the ring box out again.

Mikey and Izzy jumped off the ride and joined them. 'No waaay, he's doing it here!'

Izzy looked across at her mother and gasped in equal measures of shock and delight.

Sharon felt her cheeks colour as fellow riders

and passers-by twigged as to what was going on and started whooping and cheering.

'Sharon Taylor, for the second time today … will you marry me?'

She didn't hesitate for a moment. 'Yes … for the second time today, *yes!*

Grahame took out the white gold diamond engagement ring from its box and slid it onto her finger, pulling her and the kids into a group hug as the adoring onlookers gave them a round of applause.

I Can Sea Clearly Now

Chapter 18

September 2022

Sharon gazed out of the window of the Imperial Hotel suite. She could see the sea, which meant that Jim could see her in her wedding dress. He wouldn't have approved of the price of it, but he would have appreciated how beautiful his daughter looked. Her backcombed platinum bob showcased a twinkling crystal tiara and her ivory mermaid gown with its crystal brooch belt showcased her tiny waist. Her make-up was flawless. She was exquisite – a picture-perfect bride.

When She'd married Gary all those years ago, Sharon had worn a simple white tea dress to the registry office. It had not been the fairy-tale. There had been no veil, no tiara, no bridesmaids; but the father of the bride had been there by her side as they'd walked into the ceremony room. This time, Sharon had the fairy-tale: the wedding dress, the veil, the tiara and two bridesmaids. But, with no father of the bride, the fairy-tale would be bittersweet.

Sue joined her daughter at the window, stylishly subdued in her blush pink pencil dress, matching bolero jacket and disc fascinator hat; not just mother of the bride, she was acting father of the bride today, too. She draped an arm around Sharon's waist as they stood looking out to sea. 'He's here in spirit, love,' she said in a low voice, 'if only he could see you now. He'd be proud as punch.'

Sharon nodded, her eyes welling. She could hear his voice chastising her: *you've just paid that lass an arm and leg fer yer warpaint, don't go and feckin' cry it all off!*

A soft knock came at the room door. Trace swished toward it.

'Just to let you know, the wedding car is here,' an amiable voice resonated from out in the corridor.

'Ah. Cheers, love.' Trace closed the door and looked toward Sharon, her eyes as sparky as her smile. 'Car's here. You ready?'

Slowly, she turned in a stunning spectacle of twinkles; her dress stained with silent, invisible tears. 'I'm ready.'

The ribbon-dressed Rolls-Royce Phantom waited out in the carpark and the bridal party made their way toward it in a flurry of ivory tulle and blush pink chiffon. The August sun was scorching, but the light sea breeze took the edge off.

Trace allowed herself a gander of the dapper driver who stood debonair at the car's rear. 'Phwooooooar!' She muttered discreetly. 'I'll go in the front!'

Sharon gazed out of the car window as it made its way along Marine Parade. In the next hour she would be Mrs Murray. Mrs Sharon Murray. She thought of Tilly, Grahame's first wife. She had made this journey in Aberdeen. Met Grahame at the altar. Took his name. Given him a child. But she'd been denied the rest of her life with her boys. Sharon hadn't known her, but in that moment, she made a quiet promise to Tilly that she would love Grahame and Mikey for the both of them.

Sharon could hear the bagpipes from the main road as the car turned off it and, already, the River Yare in tears threatened to burst the banks of her perfectly made-up eyes. Moments on, the car rolled through the gate to St Nicholas church standing tall and mighty against a backdrop of cloudless, aquamarine sky. It had to be a church this time and no other church would do.

The car drew up outside the entrance. Trace, Sue, and Izzy exited the passenger nearside doors, while the chauffer opened the offside rear. Sharon took his gloved hand and stepped out of the Rolls-Royce onto the brilliantly sunlit church grounds.

Izzy and Trace stood in place first in line in the procession, while Sue stood beside Sharon in readiness to walk her down the aisle. She seemed to read her daughter's thoughts. 'I don't suppose you'd have gotten him in a suit, anyway, love. Daft bugger would've walked you down the aisle in his Crocs.'

They allowed themselves a jocular chuckle.

The piper stopped playing and Sharon's heart thrummed like a Scottish tenor drum as the chatter resonating among family, friends, colleagues, and half of Aberdeen inside quietened to hushed whispers. There followed a hubbub of heels on the church floor as the audience stood up en masse for the bride's entrance.

A brief pause followed before the church organ fired up and Izzy, angelic in her chiffon fallen shoulder gown, floated serenely down the aisle, followed by Trace – who wasn't quite as floaty or serene, but just ... well, Trace. She took her seat next to Barry on the end of the pew and greeted him with a giant smacker on the lips, so noisy it could be heard above the music.

Sue gave Sharon's arm a reassuring squeeze as they stepped inside and made their way toward the aisle. Both immediately spotted Norma sat at the back sporting her gummiest grin yet. She looked thoroughly delighted, and why not? She finally had a reason to wear that massive pink fascinator.

Sharon's adoring smile dropped somewhat as she remembered that there was every possibility Norma might 'faint' during the service.

Mick Hendry sat on the end of the pew in

front beside his wife like The Godfather; positively dripping in gold. Sand Scapes had been shortlisted for *AA Holiday Centre of the Year*. And, with his snappy designer suit, gold cufflinks, gold curb chain bracelets on both wrists and sovereign rings now on pretty much every finger, Mick was wearing his victory. It was a wonder he hadn't had all his teeth pulled out and replaced with gold ones! He looked up and gave a friendly salute as they approached.

A sea of heads turned their way as they arrived at the bottom of the aisle. Sharon's gaze drifted to the top and there he was in all his handsomeness waiting by the altar, lovely Grahame in his green tartan kilt, Prince Charlie jacket, and black bow tie. She smiled, and not just in anticipation of him having nothing on under that kilt. Mikey stood by his dad's side, adorbs in matching attire.

Pink-Hydrangea-bouquet-in-hand, Sharon took the last few steps – not merely down the aisle, but in her journey to happiness, and not in some parallel universe, but here and now. No longer need she imagine what was behind that 'hidden door' because now, she knew…
She was looking right at it.

$\mathcal{E}pilogue$

Around Twenty Minutes Later

You could've heard a pin drop in the church as Reverend King asked the question everybody dreads. 'If any person here present knows of any lawful impediment to this marriage, they should declare it now.'

A brash voice came out of nowhere. 'FACKIN' 'ELL, SHAZ! I'VE JUST 'AD A THOUGHT! MADAME CATHARINA WAS SPOT ON, WEREN'T SHE?!'

About The Author

Gem Burman

Gem Burman is a women's fiction author from Great Yarmouth, England; currently living in Norwich, England with her husband and three children. Self-published, Gem is a one-woman band with no team of professionals behind her, and no writing qualifications, just a huge  passion for storytelling and a great belief in following your dreams regardless of who you are and where you come from.

www.gemburman.com
www.facebook.com/gemburman
www.instagram.com/gemburmanauthor
www.twitter.com/gemburmanauthor

Books By This Author

A Kind Of Tragic

Rude, crude, and immensely funny!
She's the perfect poster girl for how not to be and
what not to do in life. Every day is an epic fail with
calamity around every corner. She's a dreamer. A
schemer. A complete chancer, totally winging it
with no life plan and just hoping everything will
somehow work out... but who says you can't be the
world's biggest ninny and still win?

Lizzie Bradshaw's two great loves in life are
donuts and Dan Elliott, her devilishly handsome
co-worker and hers is one brutally honest and
hilarious account of unrequited love that you do
not want to miss.

Guys like Dan Elliott wouldn't usually look twice at
women like Lizzie, let alone date them. But what if
there was a way to change the odds and turn fate
on its head, even with the supermodelesque new
starter at work also vying for Dan's affections?
(Cow!) It all seems too good to be true, but

sometimes, all is not as it seems and Lizzie might just be about to discover she can have her cake and eat it; in more ways than one!

Disclaimer: not suitable for prudes, puritans, sticks-in-the-mud, goody-goodies, and/or the easily offended. May cause laughter-induced bursts of incontinence.

Warning: Page-turner. Highly addictive. May need to put entire life on hold whilst reading.

A Kind Of Tragic Wedding

The date is set and the venue booked; everything in place for the nuptials of the future Mr & Mrs. Brian Garcia. But after a chance encounter with Dan Elliott (a.k.a Mr. Wonderful), what was all very simple and straightforward is now anything but!

Two love interests. Ninety-nine problems. One BIG decision ...

Lizzie Bradshaw is back!

A Kind Of Tragic Motherhood

The fabulously funny finale in the romantic comedy series!

They say that marriage and children are the

biggest tests of any relationship, but for Lizzie Elliott, nee Bradshaw, this must only apply to other couples; after all, she and Dan are soulmates and this is all she's ever wanted. It's a dream come true!

No. The biggest test of a relationship is when Margot Robbie's body double arrives into your husband's daily life in the shape of the breathtaking Amber Ross. She's fun, she's fabulous, and she definitely doesn't eat yoghurts with a fork! But is she dazzling enough to take the shine out of Lizzie and Dan's marriage? With Dan growing ever more distant, it certainly seems that way. Something's off; something's changed. Is it all in Lizzie's head, or might it be that she doesn't truly know the one person she thought she knew inside-out?

With two under one's to care for, madder hair than ever, a flagging marriage to save, and no time to fart, this Calamity Jane is running on empty with a full swear jar!

Printed in Great Britain
by Amazon